BARE KNUC̶...
AND N̶...

Skye Fargo look̶ ... ̶ ̶ ̶
down, all nearly s̶ ̶ ̶ ̶, with arms
and legs like the t̶ ̶ ̶ of trees.

Manning looked down at Fargo. "You've
been getting in my way," Duke lazily said.

"Guns or bare hands?" was Skye's only reply.

He hoped against hope it would be guns.
That would cut down the size between them.

Manning reached down and slowly unbuckled his belt. He slung it onto the bar. Fargo
had no choice. He unbuckled his belt as well.

Fargo had been crazy with rage about what
Manning had done to a young and innocent
girl. But now, as Manning came toward him
with his face lit by murderous joy and his huge
hands ready to kill, Fargo realized just how
crazy he was ... to fight a man who couldn't
be beaten ... and to put himself next on the
list of dead men who'd gotten in Duke Manning's way. . . .

THE TRAILSMAN

139

BUFFALO GUNS

by

Jon Sharpe

A SIGNET BOOK

SIGNET
Published by the Penguin Group
Penguin Books USA Inc., 375 Hudson Street,
New York, New York 10014, U.S.A.
Penguin Books Ltd, 27 Wrights Lane,
London W8 5TZ, England
Penguin Books Australia Ltd, Ringwood,
Victoria, Australia
Penguin Books Canada Ltd, 10 Alcorn Avenue,
Toronto, Ontario, Canada M4V 3B2
Penguin Books (N.Z.) Ltd, 182-190 Wairau Road,
Auckland 10, New Zealand

Penguin Books Ltd, Registered Offices:
Harmondsworth, Middlesex, England

First published by Signet, an imprint of New American Library,
a division of Penguin Books USA Inc.

First Printing, July, 1993
10 9 8 7 6 5 4 3 2 1

The first chapter of this book originally appeared in *Silver Fury*, the one
hundred and thirty-eighth volume in this series.

REGISTERED TRADEMARK—MARCA REGISTRADA

Printed in the United States of America

BOOKS ARE AVAILABLE AT QUANTITY DISCOUNTS WHEN USED TO PROMOTE
PRODUCTS OR SERVICES. FOR INFORMATION PLEASE WRITE TO PREMIUM MAR-
KETING DIVISION, PENGUIN BOOKS USA INC., 375 HUDSON STREET, NEW YORK,
NEW YORK 10014.

The Trailsman

Beginnings ... they bend the tree and they mark the man. Skye Fargo was born when he was eighteen. Terror was his midwife, vengeance his first cry. Killing spawned Skye Fargo, ruthless, cold-blooded murder. Out of the acrid smoke of gunpowder still hanging in the air, he rose, cried out a promise never forgotten.

The Trailsman they began to call him all across the West: searcher, scout, hunter, the man who could see where others only looked, his skills for hire but not his soul, the man who lived each day to the fullest, yet trailed each tomorrow. Skye Fargo, the Trailsman, the seeker who could take the wildness of a land and the wanting of a woman and make them his own.

Kansas Territory, 1860 . . .
a lawless tract of horizon, grass, and sky-
where some men grab what they want, when they want it—
other men's buffalo skins, money, or women.

1

The warrior sprawled on the buffalo grass and stared wide-eyed into the blank blue sky above. The afternoon sun gilded the bronze skin of the dead Indian's face. His mouth sagged open as if he could not believe his own death. A headband, its eagle feathers askew, was tangled in the brave's long, dark hair. The ragged hole of the bullet wound darkened the buckskin shirt and the handle of a tomahawk protruded from the bloody shoulder.

The tall man sat astride the black-and-white pinto and gazed down at the body. His lake blue eyes slowly and methodically scanned the scene before him, noting the trampled buffalo grass, the Indian's clothing, the wounds. Slowly he shook his head, then glanced up at the wheeling hawks. The vultures would come soon.

Skye Fargo regarded the dead man again. And he heard, inside himself, the voice that recited what he knew about what had happened. Fresh blood—a fresh kill. The brave had been dead less than an hour. The beaded moccasins—white with distinctive jagged triangles and stripes—marked him as Cheyenne. And the number of eagle feathers was a sign that he had been a respected warrior. A wide bullet wound indicated point-blank range.

Fargo dismounted and knelt on the ground for a moment, examining the coarse, trampled sod. The matted grass was too thick to make out a clear track. But, the bent and broken blades showed signs of a struggle. He followed the tracks and found the faint traces of several horses. Fargo frowned and walked back to the body, stooping over it to examine, at last, what disturbed his mind the most.

He yanked the stone tomahawk from the flesh of the warrior and wiped the blood off on the grass. Then he held the tomahawk before him and took the emblem that dangled from a buck-skin thong between his fingers. The disc was fash-ioned of buffalo leather, painted yellow with a blue circle in the center. It was a miniature of a war shield. And it was Kiowa.

Skye Fargo shook his head again, puzzled.

"Kiowa," he said out loud to himself slowly. "Killing Cheyenne." It didn't make sense, he heard the inner voice say. Kiowa had upheld the tribal treaty for twenty years. Back in 1840, the two southern tribes—the Kiowa and the Coman-che—had come north of Arrowpoint, which is what they called the Arkansas River, to hold a big powwow with the Cheyenne and Arapaho. The four tribes met, exchanged horses and gifts and promises of peace. And they had kept the treaty. At least, until now. If the tribes started fighting one another, it would be only a matter of time before a white man was caught in the crossfire. Then the killing would spill over to the settlers, too. And Cheyenne and Kiowa were some of the fiercest warriors on the plains.

Fargo held the tomahawk in his hand and regarded it again. It was carefully made. The smooth mesquite wood handle fit snugly around the chipped quartz blade. Yucca cord wrapped the grip handle, carved in curves to fit the hand. It was a fine weapon. Fargo raised it into the air and brought it down. Beautifully balanced.

The ax had not killed the Cheyenne brave. The bullet had. And the tomahawk had been left in the Indian's shoulder. No Indian would abandon this, Fargo thought, hefting the tomahawk again. Such weapons took many months to perfect. Indian warriors always conserved their weapons. Fargo had seen them pull arrows from game and from dead men in order to repair and use them again. The Kiowa who owned this tomahawk had been in a hurry, Fargo thought. Or wanted to leave a message for anyone who could read it.

Fargo stowed the tomahawk in his saddlebag and remounted the pinto. He gazed eastward across the waving tawny grass. A half a mile away, a line of white bones striped the rolling plain. Fargo had passed by the spot before he discovered the dead Cheyenne. More than thirty bison killed in one place. White hunters. It was getting to be a common sight on the Kansas prairie.

Beyond the white buffalo bones, the horizon was sharp against the September blue sky. Several miles back, still out of sight, the wagon train was following. He had led the supply train out from Independence, Missouri, along the Santa Fe Trail through Council Grove and Fort Dodge before leaving the trail and driving parallel to the Arkansas River to Fort McKinney. It had been an unremarkable trip, Fargo thought. Until now.

He glanced at the lowering sun and calculated how much daylight he'd have once the wagons caught up with him. If he pushed their pace, the wagons would arrive at Fort McKinney just after nightfall, a day earlier than expected.

Fargo decided to search for tracks before he rejoined the wagons. He took the pinto in an ever-widening spiral around the dead Indian. Soon he found what he was looking for.

Indistinct horses' hooves again. And two deep lines of torn sod—the trail of a travois—traveling north to south, heading toward the Arkansas River.

Now what was the Cheyenne brave, or his killers, hauling on a travois? Fargo chewed on that question as he galloped back to the wagon train.

The dozen clapboard buildings comprising Fort McKinney clustered around a wide and dusty parade ground, on a gentle bluff overlooking the Arkansas River. Like most forts in the West, it didn't have a wall around it and had never been attacked. Instead, it served as a staging base for military operations in the surrounding countryside.

In the five years since the fort has been established, a town had sprung up around it, attracted by the comforting prospect of military protection. The collection of sod houses and yellow lumber buildings sprawled chaotically on the riverbank.

The last red of the autumn sunset was fading to purple as Fargo brought the wagons to a halt in front of the quartermaster's storehouse. A skinny private, just a kid, scurried forward, clicked his heels, and saluted smartly.

"Where's the quartermaster?" Fargo asked. Before the kid had a chance to answer, a grizzled second lieutenant emerged carrying a lantern. Fargo dismounted and handed over the requisition order.

"I'll need to check the supplies against the list before I can pay you," the lieutenant said. "Army regulations. Going by the book."

They had never held him up to take inventory before. Fargo started to protest, then thought better of it. "While you're doing that, where's Colonel Straver? I need a word with him."

Fargo and Colonel Straver went way back. Straver was one of the few military men Fargo respected—he was disciplined, forthright, and sensible. But he was also a man who hadn't lost his independence after a long career in the military. It would be prudent to alert the colonel about the dead warrior he had seen on the prairie. If the peace between the Kiowa and the Cheyenne was about to be broken by full-scale war, then Straver would want to know about it.

"Gone," the quartermaster said absentmindedly, as he perused the list of supplies.

"Where?"

"Hmm?" The lieutenant glanced up. "Oh, yes. The colonel has gone west with the troops to follow those renegades that have been jumping the stagecoaches south of Denver City. They won't be back for two weeks. There's hardly anybody left here at Fort McKinney."

Fargo bit his lip in thought. Troops gone for two weeks. If the Cheyenne and the Kiowa launched into a full-scale war, even against each other, there would be a panic in the town. If things got bad, the commanding officer at the fort would have to organize the townsfolk to protect themselves. That would take some real leadership.

"Who's in command?"

"Major Brimwell," the quartermaster answered. He looked up at the line of fifteen wagons. "Major Brimwell is the reason I have to go by the book here." Fargo heard the impatience in the lieutenant's voice. "Otherwise, I'd just pay you and be done with it. In any case, I'll be finished inventory here in about an hour," he said. "You'll find the major in the officers' quarters."

"Fine," Fargo said. "The wagons are yours, except the last one over there." Fargo pointed to a wide-bodied mountain wagon filled with wooden crates.

The lieutenant nodded. "Just out of curiosity, what's in it?"

"Petticoats," Fargo said with a smile. "Lace petticoats and things like that. Hundreds of 'em."

The quartermaster chuckled.

"You must be doing a job for The Gilded Cage."

"Yep," Fargo said. "Can't beat the pay." He moved off toward the officers' quarters. He was thinking of Sylvia. After he had spoken to the commanding officer, he would make his delivery to The Gilded Cage. And then enjoy his reward.

A smile of anticipation still lingered on Fargo's face as he crossed the threshold of the officers' quarters and found Major Brimwell at a card game with several officers.

The major threw down his hand as Fargo approached.

"I'm having no luck tonight," he complained. "Who are you, sir? What brings you here?"

"I brought in the supply wagons," Fargo said, taking an empty chair at the major's elbow as they watched the game finish. "I need to talk to you."

The major rose and ushered him into a small, bare office. Brimwell took a seat behind the desk and poured two shot glasses of bourbon, sliding one across to Fargo.

"I saw something ten miles east of here you should know about," Fargo said.

"Ten miles east?" the major repeated. "At Reggio's Trading Post?" Fargo thought of the hunchbacked trader, Reggio, and his lively trading post on the river. After his business here and at The Gilded Cage, Fargo had to pay a visit to Reggio to deliver the cash payment he was carrying in the inside pocket of his coat.

"No," Fargo said. "Not on the river. North of there a few miles, on the prairie. I found a dead Cheyenne . . ."

"So?" Brimwell cut in impatiently. He poured himself another shot and downed it. "What's one more dead savage?"

"He'd been shot at close range. And he had a Kiowa tomahawk embedded in his shoulder."

The major glared across the desk at Fargo. "You interrupted my card game, sir, to tell me that?"

Fargo shrugged. The man was stupid. And without curiosity. Or imagination. Brimwell was everything Fargo hated about the military. Follow the rules. Don't ask questions. Don't use your brain. That's what military life did to some men.

The weaker ones anyway. The stronger ones, like Colonel Straver, were tempered by it, hardened like fine steel which never lost its edge. But Brimwell was not one of those.

"A Kiowa tomahawk in a Cheyenne brave," Fargo repeated slowly, trying to summon patience and keep his temper in check. "Those two tribes have had an unbroken treaty for twenty years. And now, there might be war between them."

The major leaned forward.

"Now I understand, sir," he said, thumping the table with his knuckles. "That's wonderful news! If the Kiowa and the Cheyenne are going to butcher each other, it will save us a hell of a lot of time. Much faster than finding the provocation to kill those redskins ourselves. This is the best news I've heard since I've been out here in this godforsaken country. Indians slaughtering Indians! I'll drink to that!" The major poured himself another shot and refilled Fargo's glass. He clinked his glass to Fargo's, which sat on the desk, before draining his.

"Wonderful news," he said, wheezing and putting down the glass.

Fargo watched the major. Stupid. Damn stupid, he thought. The kind of man who didn't see danger coming straight at him. Until it was too late.

"There's something else," Fargo said. He didn't like Major Brimwell. And with every moment that passed, he liked him even less. "No Kiowa would leave a good tomahawk in an enemy's shoulder. Unless he's in a hurry to get away. Or he wants to leave a message."

The major shrugged.

"That seems to me a petty detail, sir," he said.

"Nothing to concern yourself with. Indians leave their weapons all over the place. All over the place." The major's voice was slurred from the bourbon.

"No," Fargo said slowly. "They don't. There's something very strange about this to my way of thinking."

"Why, there's nothing strange at all," Brimwell said. "One barbarian slays another. Nothing strange . . ." The major hiccupped loudly. "I'd say, sir, that the only thing strange *is* your way of thinking. In fact, I'd say you think mighty strangely. You think, sir, like an Indian!" The major hiccupped again.

"I guess I do," Fargo said, rising to leave. "I guess I do at that."

It was his fifteenth and final trip through the crowded bar of The Gilded Cage. The wagon was nearly unloaded. Fargo balanced a wooden crate on his shoulder. Petticoats were surprisingly heavy.

"Mr. Fargo!" the bartender called as he passed by.

Fargo paused, resting the crate against the bar. The bartender leaned across and spoke low.

"What?" Fargo called out, not catching the man's words. "It's noisy as a calf corral in here!"

The bartender leaned closer until he spoke into Fargo's ear. "Somebody's been asking about you." Fargo nodded and the bartender's large, watery eyes blinked a few times.

"What about me?"

"Wanted to know what your name is. Let slip he'd heard you were coming into town with wagons. Real surprised to find you here. Said he expected you'd be in tomorrow. He asked one of the girls and she didn't like his tone. She just told me while she was getting him another drink."

Fargo nodded again.

"Which one is he?"

"Sitting over against the wall by the door," the bartender said, careful not to point or to let his watery eyes stray in that direction and reveal the subject of their conversation if the man happened to be watching them. "The one with the big fur cap on. Looks like a mean son of a bitch."

"I'll look him over," Fargo said. "And I'll watch my back. Thanks for the tip."

The bartender turned to another customer and Fargo lifted the crate onto his shoulder again. He made his way to the staircase and climbed halfway up. Then he turned, as if tired, and rested the crate against the banister. He wiped his forehead with one sleeve as his eyes swept the room.

The Gilded Cage was jammed with customers, standing at the bar, playing cards, drinking at the tables. There was a familiar figure at the piano, Fargo noted. He'd have a talk with Mandy later.

Just as he turned back, he let his eyes sweep the wall near the door. The man was there all right, he thought, as he lifted the crate and continued up the stair. An ugly, burly bastard with a thick brown beard and a tattered fur cap. Sitting alone next to the door, back to the wall. A man didn't usually take that position unless he was planning to cause some trouble and make a quick escape. And he'd been watching Fargo with his beady black eyes. On the other hand, it could be nothing, Fargo thought. But he knew the man was up to no good. He'd get to the bottom of it

18

later. But first, a more pleasant task. He climbed the final stair.

He could hear their voices all the way from the other end of the hall. He made his way to the end of the papered corridor and pushed open a door, entering and depositing the crate onto the floor. The room was a blizzard of lace, crinoline, and frills. Fluffy piles of petticoats, most of them white and all of them ruffled and flounced, covered the chairs and sofas of the drawing room. He bent down and pried the top off the last crate.

"Oh, Skye you darling!"

A pert brunette named Bernadette flung her arms around him when she saw the pink undergarments in the last crate, and the other girls squealed and gathered around. Fargo gave Bernadette a squeeze, enjoying her soft curves. She kissed him quickly and wriggled from his grasp to kneel down beside the newly opened box. In a moment the air was a fountain of flying lace as she pulled the lingerie from the crate and tossed them about the room to the other girls.

So many girls ran to and fro, in various stages of undress, that Fargo had a hard time counting them all. Maybe fifteen, he concluded. And each of them, every single one, was screeching with delight. Fargo covered his ears and uttered a complaint, but no one heard him above the din.

He kept his hands over his ears and watched as a curvaceous redhead, packed into a tight lavender corset which pressed her large breasts upward, struggled out of a bright yellow petticoat. A willowy brunette sitting on a horsehair couch extended one long leg and slipped her pointed toe into a red garter, pulling it up onto her slender thigh. She glanced up, noted Fargo's appreciative gaze, and smiled back. But her attention was distracted immediately by a plump blonde modeling an extravagantly lacy petticoat which billowed about her. Fargo turned away and descended the stairs, his ears ringing. He wondered where Sylvia was keeping herself.

As he descended the staircase, out of the corner of his eye Fargo saw the man beside the door come slowly to his feet. Fargo flexed his right hand, ready to turn and draw. He continued down, but the man simply stood, not making a move. By the time he reached the floor, the man was out of sight again, hidden by the crowd standing at the bar. He'd have to keep an eye out.

All the tables were filled. Some of the girls had already come downstairs, and Fargo was amused to see that their skirts were vastly inflated by an extravagance of petticoats underneath.

Fargo glanced around the jammed room, but didn't see Sylvia anywhere, so he ordered a beer from the bartender.

"I saw him," Fargo said as he paid. "Anybody know him?"

"I asked a couple of the other girls," the bartender said. "Nobody's seen him around here before."

"He's a buffalo hunter, by the looks of him."

"And a mean one," the bartender said, nodding.

Fargo took a swig of the beer and searched his memory for the man's face. He was sure he had never seen him before. If he was following Fargo, he had probably been sent by somebody else. But who? And why?

Fargo turned to look out at the crowd. Mandy

was still the piano man. He pushed his way to a chair beside the battered upright piano. Mandy glanced at him, then smiled broadly in recognition, his white teeth bright in his black face.

"Why, lawdsy, Mr. Fargo," Mandy said. "Miss Sylvia didn't tell me it was you bringing those underthings for the ladies. I should have known it."

His big hands moved faultlessly over the black-and-white keys.

"How have you been, Mandy?" Fargo said. He glanced toward the door again. He could see over the heads of the men sitting at the tables. He was still there. Still standing against the wall. Still watching.

"Never better."

"And business?"

"I guess you haven't heard the news," Mandy said, shaking his head in mock sorrow, trying to suppress his smile. "Miss Sylvia, she's been doing better than ever. Making so much money, she hardly knows what to do with it. 'Cept now she's got that all figured out."

"And what's that?"

"Why, she's closing down The Gilded Cage. At the end of the month. She's buying a ranch up Nebraska way. And I aim to work on it. That's why she's been buying all those things for the girls. To set them up right. Some of 'em are getting hitched. Some of the others will continue gaming, I reckon. It's a sad thing, closing down The Gilded Cage."

"It's a terrible thing," Fargo agreed. "I'll bet there's a lot of serious mourning going on over at Fort McKinney. But, where is Sylvia? I haven't seen her yet."

"Oh, she's around," said Mandy, swiveling his head.

Just then, a door opened to the side of the bar. Fargo stood up as a small figure emerged. Dressed in a flamboyant red dress with two red ostrich feathers crowning her head, Sylvia Roland—the Silver Sparrow—made her grand entrance.

She was small, hardly bigger than a half-grown girl, but roundly shaped. Her ash blond hair fell in perfect ringlets down her back, and her dress was cut low to reveal a creamy neck and two beautifully rounded breasts above a tiny waist. Fargo watched as the bartender hoisted Sylvia onto the bar. She got to her feet and walked the length of it, stepping gracefully over the glasses and bottles. Her fringed skirt was cut to reveal her slender ankles and her red leather laced boots. She paused to chat and laugh with the men at her feet. They toasted her as she made her way to the end of the bar and back.

She spotted Fargo immediately and let out a yell. The bartender swung her down, and she quickly bustled over to the piano.

"You're here at last!" she said as Fargo bent over to kiss her. Her mouth was as sweet as honey, as sweet as he remembered, and he felt her surprisingly strong arms reach up to embrace him. Fargo grinned and lifted her off her feet.

"Put me down!" she said, pretending to struggle in his embrace. "What will my customers think?"

Indeed, many of the men sitting at the tables around the piano had turned to watch them. And with barely disguised envy. The Silver Sparrow made it a rule never to cavort with the customers. The sole exception was Skye Fargo.

Fargo's eyes flickered toward the door. Still there. Still watching.

"They'll think we haven't seen each other for a long time," Fargo said, nuzzling her fragrant hair. He held her with one arm only. His other hand hung loose, near his Colt.

"And that's the truth," she said. "But, later. Put me down. I have to maintain some kind of dignity." Fargo grinned. He turned and hoisted her on top of the piano, turning around again quickly. The man beside the door hadn't moved.

"You can't come down until you sing," Fargo teased. The tables around them fell silent as the customers scraped their chairs against the wooden floor so they could see better. Several voices called out excitedly for a song from Sylvia. Then a hush fell on the room.

Just as Mandy struck the opening chords, there was a sudden movement beside the door. Fargo leapt aside as the bullet whizzed by him. Piano wire twanged as it hit the upright. Fargo swept Sylvia off the piano, pushing her onto the floor where she'd be out of the line of fire. The men in the bar scrambled for cover under the tables, behind the bar.

Fargo turned and drew as a second shot exploded. Mandy cried out and slumped down, crashing onto the keyboard, a bullet wound in his back.

Fargo felt the black rage swell inside him, a fury so deep it darkened the room until he saw only the brown-bearded bastard standing beside the door, pistol raised, preparing to fire again. Everything moved in slow motion as Fargo raised his pistol, noting the man's beady eyes and thick brow. Fargo squeezed the trigger, catching him in the shoulder. He wanted to keep the man alive so he could get a few questions out of him.

The man recoiled and his pistol fired again, the shot flying wide. His pistol dropped from his hand. Fargo continued to advance, Colt raised. Fear blazed in the man's eyes as he clutched his wounded shoulder. He looked to the floor where his pistol had fallen. Suddenly he threw himself onto it, scrambling to get ahold of the weapon with his good hand. Fargo had reached him and grabbed him by the collar when the man's pistol went off.

The body jerked with the impact, then relaxed.

Fargo swore and rolled the body face up. The shot had caught him dead center in the chest. The face was slack, eyes lifeless. Fargo swore again. He would get no answers out of this one.

Suddenly Sylvia was beside him, tears streaking her face. She clutched Fargo's arm.

"Who would want to kill . . . to kill Mandy?" she sobbed. The room began to buzz as the customers got to their feet again and gathered around.

"I don't know," Fargo said, looking down at the man lying before him.

An innocent man was dead. And the murderer could answer no questions.

Fargo knew the bullets had been intended for him. He had no doubt of that. But for the moment, he thought, as he looked around the crowded room, he'd keep his thoughts to himself.

2

Fargo didn't waste time looking at the dead man. Instead, he backed up and watched the crowd as it emerged hesitantly from beneath the tables. The brown-bearded stranger might have been with somebody. And that somebody might fire on him again before he knew what was happening. He'd seen it happen before.

But the customers were talking and craning their necks to see the dead man. No one looked suspicious. No one made a fast move. After a few moments, Fargo turned his attention back to the body before him. But he stayed on guard.

Fargo knelt quickly and rifled through the man's pockets, looking for a clue. The man's jacket was of badly tanned hide, darkened with grime and what looked like bloodstains. In the pockets Fargo found a few silver coins, a folding knife, and four small pieces of carved bone, two plain and two with a dark band around the middle. Indian, he thought, wondering what they were used for. He pocketed the pieces of bone, replaced everything else, and straightened up.

The batwing doors swung open, and a flushed-faced red-haired man strode in. A brightly polished star was pinned on his vest. He stopped when he saw Fargo, and his hand twitched over his pistol, his eyes wary of trouble.

Fargo touched the brim of his hat.

"This one fired on the piano player," Fargo said, gesturing over his shoulder. He was aware of the crowd pressing in around him, listening to every word.

"Got him, too," the sheriff said, his eyes taking in Sylvia standing over Mandy's body. "Damn shame." He looked down. "You shoot him?"

Fargo nodded.

"I tried to wing him, but he fell on his pistol."

The sheriff cocked his head as he looked down at the dead man. He glanced up at Fargo.

"The name's Smythe. Who are you?"

"Fargo. Skye Fargo."

Smythe's red brows shot up, and a low buzz began in the room as the crowd repeated Fargo's name.

"You the one they call the Trailsman?"

Fargo nodded.

"I'll be damned," Smythe said, his voice taking on a note of awed respect. "Always wanted to get a look at you. If half the things I heard about you are true . . . Well, maybe you can tell me what this is about?"

Fargo shook his head. "No idea," he said.

"Never seen him around here before. Who is he?" The sheriff toed the body thoughtfully.

Fargo shrugged. "Looks like a buffalo hunter."

"Anybody here know this son of a bitch?" the sheriff asked. Several of the crowd murmured no.

"I didn't realize Mandy had any enemies," the sheriff said, shaking his head. "I guess Sylvia will want to take care of Mandy in a proper fashion.

Meanwhile, I'd be obliged, Mr. Fargo, if you help me get this body out of The Gilded Cage."

Fargo nodded and they each grabbed a leg and dragged the bulky dead man through the doors and out onto the boardwalk. The night wind was cool and a quarter moon was rising. They pulled the corpse off to one side of the saloon, depositing it near a wagon. Smythe covered it with a canvas tarp.

"I'll tell Mr. Flyte where to pick this one up," the sheriff said, as if speaking to himself. Fargo guessed that Mr. Flyte would be the town undertaker. "I still can't figure out why . . ."

"He wasn't shooting at Mandy," Fargo broke in. The sheriff paused and gazed at him, his eyes sharp. "He was aiming at me. Somebody must have sent him. I didn't want to share my suspicions in front of everybody in town."

"Wise. Always figure a bastard's got friends," Smythe said. "But who's got a grudge against the Trailsman?"

"Could be any of a hundred men," Fargo said. "I've made some enemies over the years."

"Bet you have," Smythe said.

"I found these in his pocket." Fargo held the pieces of carved bone on his palm, moving them into the light streaming out of the saloon window. Smythe bent over and examined them.

"Indian," he muttered. "But I'll be damned if I know what they are." He straightened up again and looked Fargo up and down. "You'd better keep your eyes open. Whoever it is will try again. 'Long as you're in town, I'd like to stand you for a drink."

"Sure," Fargo said. "I figure I'll go back inside

for a while and show myself. Then I'll ride out of town. I've got some business east of here at Reggio's Trading Post. If that brown beard had a friend with him, then he'll follow. He'll be easier to pick off if I find him tracking me across the open prairie at night than if he's standing in the middle of a crowd."

Smythe nodded thoughtfully. "Sounds like a good plan. I'll watch your tail," he said. After you ride out, I'll follow whoever takes out after you. Two against one. I like those odds better."

"Much obliged," Fargo said. They pushed through the batwing doors again.

One quick beer and ten minutes later, Sylvia was pouting.

"Don't tell me my reward's going to expire if I don't collect it now," Fargo murmured in her ear. He nibbled on her earlobe. She shook her head, making her blond ringlets bounce over her bare shoulders.

"Damn you, Skye," she said, giggling. "I got my hopes up for a rousing good night with you and off you go. But," her voice took on a serious note, "I do understand. Just get back here soon."

During their drink, Fargo and Smythe had propped themselves against the bar, covertly observing the crowded room. Fargo was almost certain that no one was watching them. Could the murderer have come alone? Still, it was better to take precautions.

Fargo took Sylvia in his arms quickly and kissed her goodbye, enjoying the sweet familiar taste of her mouth and the faint smell of her perfume. Damn it. He'd rather be spending the night with her than riding out.

He nodded to Smythe and exited. Outside, he mounted his black-and-white pinto and galloped east down the moonlit street, which seemed to lead straight to the rising moon.

The lone horseman paused at the top of the swell and seemed unsure as to which way to ride. All around, the seemingly endless prairie was dark silver and silent under the pale light of the moon. Fargo, kneeling in a gully, the pinto lying down beside him, narrowed his eyes as he watched the figure.

The man on the horse waved his arm above his head slowly. Once. Twice. Three times. Fargo was sure then that it was Smythe. He rose to his feet and the pinto got up with a snort. The figure sighted them then and galloped down the rise.

"Nobody followed you," Smythe said, drawing near. "I watched like a hawk."

"Then the brown beard was alone," Fargo said. "Wish I knew who sent him."

"You riding back to town?" Smythe asked.

"No. I've got some business at Reggio's Trading Post. I'll be back through town in a couple of days." Fargo was eager to get rid of the cash that he was delivering to the trading post. Seven thousand dollars of somebody else's money was buttoned in a breast pocket inside his jacket.

"Well, I'll be heading back then," Smythe said.

"By the way," Fargo said, "you ought to know you've got some Indian trouble brewing."

"What's that?"

"I found a Cheyenne warrior with a Kiowa hatchet in him."

"Oh God," Smythe said. "If they start up a tribal

war . . ." His voice trailed off, and Fargo knew he was imagining the bloodshed—Indian and white—that might ensue if the tribes started a full-scale war. "That's worrisome," Smythe concluded after a long silence. "Of course, that's more the army's department than mine."

"Straver's gone west," Fargo said. "So, I alerted Brimwell. I don't think he got the message."

"Brimwell? That horse's ass!" Smythe spat. "He couldn't comprehend getting scalped if his pate was dangling in front of his own nose! Thanks for the warning. I'll let my posse know in case we need to go on the defensive."

They bid goodbye, and Fargo continued east in a loping canter through the darkness.

A half hour later, he galloped over a rise and saw faint red embers of a campfire nearly invisible at the bottom of a draw, several hundred yards before him. It was so well hidden, he could easily have ridden by without noticing. Fargo pulled the pinto up short and sat looking down.

His keen eyes found the form of a hobbled horse and a loaded travois nearby. A rumpled blanket lay beside the fire, barely visible in the dull red glow. There was no one in sight. Fargo guessed it was an Indian traveling alone. The brave had heard hoofbeats coming and had slipped away into the darkness. He was probably very close even now. Fargo glanced at the bushes near him and thought he detected a slight movement.

"Friend," Fargo said in Algonquian, a language common to many of the tribes of the plains. "Riding through the night. My name is Skye Fargo. Friend of Indians."

The bushes suddenly rustled as the Indian rushed forward. Fargo drew his Colt and was about to fire just as he heard his name being called.

"Skye! Skye!" The voice was familiar, and he tried to place it. The Indian slowed and approached the pinto.

"Skye! It is I! Yellow Dog! From the Cheyenne."

Fargo laughed and dismounted, taking the brave's outstretched hand. The Indian shook it solemnly for a very long time, in imitation of the way he had seen white men greet one another.

"Yellow Dog!" Fargo said, clapping him on the shoulder. "I haven't seen you for many years. Why are you away from your tribe?"

"I am traveling to the trading post on the river," said the Indian. "I have many fall buffalo robes to sell. Fine furs, thick with the coming of winter. Tomorrow I will trade."

"I'm heading to the trading post, too," said Fargo in the Cheyenne's language.

"Come share my fire and food," said Yellow Dog. "We go together."

By midnight, they had eaten well of the Indian's jerky and berries. Fargo brewed a pot of coffee, and they sat sipping it from two tin mugs. Fargo had asked Yellow Dog all the news of his small band of Cheyenne.

Over the years, Fargo had had many occasions to do battle with the Cheyenne. They were fierce warriors. But he had made friends with some of them, too.

He had met Yellow Dog's tribe years before. Unbeknownst to Fargo, a buffalo stampede had destroyed the Cheyenne village and scattered the people. He had come upon a tiny Indian girl, nearly dead from hunger and thirst, wandering lost on the prairie.

For a full day, she had resisted Fargo's rescue, hiding in a ravine and throwing stones at him. For a while he tried to wait her out. Finally he lassoed her. She was a little wildcat, scratching and spitting with fury. In order to save her life, he tied her up and forced her to eat and drink water. When he had returned her to the tribe, he found out she was only six. And her name was Ten Claws, daughter of the Chief Broken Bow and youngest sister of Yellow Dog.

The small band of Cheyenne had been grateful to him and he remained with them for a week, feasting on buffalo and sleeping in the open air since their tepees had been destroyed by the stampede. He had often wondered if he would encounter Broken Bow's band again.

"How is Ten Claws?" Fargo asked. "I hope she is still scratching?"

Yellow Dog laughed.

"Now she is grown. Sixteen summers. You would not know her. She is still fierce, yes. But woman's fierceness."

Fargo heard the pride in Yellow Dog's voice as he spoke of his sister.

"And your father?"

"Broken Bow is old. Fight is almost gone from him now. It is time for . . ."

Yellow Dog's voice stopped abruptly. Fargo knew what he had been about to say. It was time for Broken Bow to step aside. It was time for Yellow Dog to be chief. Fargo guessed that Yellow Dog was trying to suppress his eagerness and his ambition, considered by Indians unseemly. And he guessed that Yellow Dog volunteered to take the pelts to the trading post in order to be away from the village and away from the reminders that he was not yet chief.

"Winter will come when it is ready," Fargo said. He knew that Yellow Dog would understand his message. It would soon be winter for Broken Bow. Yellow Dog must be patient for the change of the seasons.

"You are wise. You speak as one of us," Yellow Dog said, looking across the dying fire at Fargo.

"Part of me is Indian," Fargo said.

"The spirit part," Yellow Dog added, "and your tongue."

Fargo laughed. Yellow Dog laughed, too, then suddenly raised his hand for silence. Fargo listened to the night. The call of a burrowing owl. And the yip of coyote several miles distant. Nearer, the faint hiss of the grasses stirred by the breeze. Nothing more. Fargo and Yellow Dog sat listening for a long time.

"We will sleep now," Yellow Dog said. "We will not need the fire tonight."

"Yellow Dog is cautious," Fargo said as he watched the brave begin to smother the last of the embers with dirt. "This afternoon, I saw a dead Cheyenne brave. A Kiowa tomahawk was in his shoulder."

Yellow Dog's hands paused, then resumed burying the fire.

"Yes," he said softly. "We have seen this, too. Many times."

"Why?" There was a long pause as Yellow Dog continued putting out the fire.

"Our old friends, Kiowa braves, ride north

across the water called Arrowhead," Yellow Dog said. "We do not see them, but they kill our braves riding alone. They take buffalo skins. They leave their Kiowa arrows and tomahawks. One of them left his medicine bundle! He must have been mad to leave his most sacred possession on the body of a slain enemy! Sometimes they take scalps, too. Sometimes they don't. They are mad. Our old friends must want war. I say kill the Kiowa. But Broken Bow, the fight has gone out of him. He is old. He is puzzled. He says he does not believe our friends want war. I say kill! Kill the Kiowa! They have broken the old treaty of the four tribes."

Yellow Dog squatted in silence. The fire was buried now under a pile of dry earth. The cold moonlight washed the clearing.

"Let us take turns sleeping," Fargo said at last. Yellow Dog grunted and Fargo knew he was relieved. The delicate matter of Indian etiquette dictated that Yellow Dog considered Fargo a guest at his campfire. A brave would never ask a guest to help keep watch. He had been relieved at Fargo's offer.

"You look out first," Yellow Dog said, offering his guest the easier first watch.

Fargo watched half the night, then woke Yellow Dog to take over. He fell into his bedroll gratefully and didn't stir until the morning light.

Yellow Dog laid a hot fire of buffalo chips while Fargo washed up at the creek. Fargo fried strips of bacon, then softened some hardtack in the grease. They washed it down with coffee. Yellow Dog smacked his lips at the unaccustomed food.

Fargo made a present of a big hunk of bacon.

Yellow Dog wrapped it carefully in buckskin and stowed it among the packages on his travois strapped to the top of a huge mound of buffalo skins. Then Yellow Dog opened one of his leather pouches and strewed trinkets on a skin, indicating that Fargo was to choose. Fargo picked two shell necklaces. They would please Sylvia, he thought, putting them into his saddlebag. Yellow Dog adjusted the lashings on his loaded travois.

"That's a fine load of skins you have there," Fargo said, walking over to inspect them. The thick buffalo pelts had been expertly tanned. Fargo saw that Yellow Dog had several dozen strapped to the travois. Enough to pay for half a dozen horses. A small fortune. He turned back one of the skins to examine the leather.

"Fur is good this year," Yellow Dog said. "Cheyenne braves kill many buffalo. Squaws scrape many hides." His voice grew somber. "But Kiowa steal. Last week one of our hunting parties came upon Kiowa hunters. They had many buffalo robes. But they said they killed the buffalo. They lie. The Kiowa lie. But one buffalo looks like another buffalo."

Fargo glanced up at him.

"You sure it's the Kiowa stealing your skins?" Yellow Dog shrugged. Fargo looked down at the robes again. "Mark them," Fargo said.

"What?"

"I said, mark the skins of the Cheyenne," Fargo said. He pulled the knife from his ankle sheath. "I'll show you what I mean."

Fargo used the point of his blade to puncture three small holes in the center of the buffalo robe. They were hardly visible unless you knew where to look. Yellow Dog watched and then smiled slowly.

"Three holes will be the sign of the Cheyenne robes," Yellow Dog said. "Then when we find Kiowa with our robes . . ."

"You'll have proof," Fargo said.

They mounted and rode out, traveling slowly because of the loaded travois. The dew on the grasses sparkled in the morning sun. They rode for several hours in silence. They passed a dried buffalo wallow and Yellow Dog drew alongside.

"This year the buffalo gods heard our prayers," Yellow Dog said. "Big herds came to us this summer. Many bulls. And now coats are getting thick for winter already. We killed so many last week that the whole tribe, even the children, are busy with the hides and meat. We will have a warm winter. Not like before."

"Before?" Fargo said. They were riding a very gradual descent toward the Arkansas River. Fargo could see the line of cottonwoods several miles ahead.

"Buffalo does not always come to us now," Yellow Dog said. "They are afraid because white men shoot so many. Used to be just one white hunter in these parts. Duke Manning and his men. But now, many others come. They bring soft white men from the East sometimes, too. So, last year and for five years, the buffalo did not come this way." Fargo heard the sadness in Yellow Dog's voice. The winters without food had been hard ones, obviously.

Buffalo migrated north with the spring and then south during the autumn. The herds usually followed the same path every year. Fargo remembered hearing other Indians say that with the coming of the white man the buffalo migrations had changed. Now, the Indians never knew, from one year to the next, where the buffalo would be. And missing them could mean a hungry winter for the tribe.

"But this year, the buffalo came back to us," Yellow Dog said, joy in his words. "So, we are happy. Plenty to eat. Fresh meat and pemmican. Many thick robes. New tepees, each made of ten buffalo. Much trading."

The green line of cottonwood trees was closer now, etched in the pale straw color of the autumn grasses. Fargo saw the glint of water beyond the trees. There beside the river was Reggio's Trading Post. Fargo could see the dark outline of it from a long way away.

Fargo and Yellow Dog rode into the front yard of the trading post. The long low mud walls of the building were broken by a few small wood-framed windows. Above the open door was a hand-lettered sign which read: REGGIO'S TRADING POST. HORSES AND IMPLEMENTS. FURS, DRY GOODS, BLANKETS. ALL TRIBES WELCOME.

Off to one side was a large corral and a series of holding pens. There were several dozen horses inside, several good ones, Fargo saw immediately. Inside the corral, a kid was trying to mount a wild Appaloosa and not having much luck. A half-dozen men hung over the railed fence to watch the fun, and several Indians stood nearby.

Beyond the corral was a bare muddy slope down to the Arkansas River where a flatboat was tied to a rickety dock. Most trading posts were located on rivers in order to move their goods quickly to markets. Dodge City was eighty miles downriver.

Fargo had stopped by the post a month before and had met Reggio for the first time. It was then that the trader had talked him into bringing the seven thousand dollars back from the bank in Dodge City. The trader offered him a thousand dollars to do it if he kept his mouth shut. And no questions. Fargo had been on the verge of asking why Reggio didn't have the money brought upriver on the flatboat. But since he had been planning to bring the wagon train for the army and the petticoats for the doves at The Gilded Cage, he figured it was easy money.

But now that somebody was after him—the brown-bearded man and whoever sent him—Fargo realized he'd need to ask questions before he delivered the money to Reggio. Just then, the trader appeared in the doorway. He sighted Yellow Dog and Fargo sitting astride their mounts and his twisted face broke out in a wide grin. He hurried out into the open and limped across the yard.

Reggio's feet twisted inward as he walked and his short arms dangled at his side. A large hump on his back pushed his head forward and to one side, so that he seemed always to be looking up quizzically. His thick brown hair was disheveled and his brown eyes wide.

"Mr. Fargo! Mr. Fargo!" he called out as he reached them. "What a relief you've come! You're a day earlier than I expected. Please, tie up your horse and come inside."

Then Reggio turned to Yellow Dog and spoke to him in Algonquian. "And you, Dog. Have you brought me more bones? **More** of those mangy flea-bitten skins you try to sell me?"

Yellow Dog simply smiled. "The trader is always telling jokes," the brave said to Fargo.

They tethered the horses, and Fargo followed Reggio inside as Yellow Dog began to unload his goods. Reggio took Fargo into a small room and closed the door behind them.

"Have you got my money with you?" Reggio asked, rubbing his hands together. "Is it safe? I need that money. I need it bad."

"It's safe," Fargo said. "But first I want some questions answered."

"What kind of questions?" Reggio asked suspiciously, his bushy brows lowering. He paced back and forth, dragging one foot across the wide planked floor. "We said no questions. That was part of the deal."

"Someone tried to kill me," Fargo said. "Tried to shoot me last night at The Gilded Cage. That changes the deal."

"Oh," Reggio said. He dropped heavily into a chair. "Maybe you have enemies. A big man like you, with your reputation . . ."

"Maybe," Fargo said. "But I think you know more about this than you're letting on. You didn't want to send this money upriver with the flatboat. Why?"

Reggio sighed.

"That payment comes from the bank at Dodge City every two months," he said reluctantly. "It's always come by boat. But four months ago, the barge was ambushed. All three men were killed, and the money was taken. It happened again two months later. So, I asked you to take it overland."

He sounded tired. "Maybe that shooting had to do with the money."

"Or it could be incidental," Fargo said. "If he wanted the money, he'd have ambushed me in a dark alley. Or out on the plains. No, he was just shooting to kill. But the question is, why? Maybe somebody's trying to scare you, Reggio. Or frighten off anybody you employ."

"Well, it's working," Reggio said. "I used to have two-dozen men working here. Since the flatboat ambushes, they've all quit one by one. Now I've got a bookkeeper and a stable boy. That's it. Makes it hard to run the place."

Fargo nodded.

"The next question is, who knew that I was bringing the payment back to you?"

Reggio hesitated for a brief instant. Fargo could see the thoughtfulness in his eyes.

"Nobody knew," he said at last. "Nobody who could tell anybody else."

"But that means somebody knew," Fargo said, impatience in his voice. Clearly Reggio was hiding something.

"Nobody!" Reggio shouted, sudden anger blazing in his brown eyes. "You hear me? I said nobody! Enough questions!"

Fargo reached inside his pocket and pulled out the packet of cash, depositing it on the table. Reggio swept it up and tore it open, counting the bills hastily. He peeled off a handful of them, thrust them at Fargo and stormed out of the room, slamming the door behind him. Fargo wondered why the hunchback had suddenly become so touchy.

Fargo shook his head in puzzlement. Reggio had implied that somebody knew about the overland delivery. But somebody who didn't talk to anyone. What the hell was going on here? He rose and went into the large central room, mulling over their conversation.

The room was jammed with goods to buy or trade. A line of burlap sacks of flour and sugar as well as cracker and pickle barrels stood along one side, surmounted by shelves which held two coffee bean grinders, brightly colored cans, jars of twisted peppermint sticks, silk pincushions, Indian pottery water jars and piles of folded blankets and calico. Hanging from the round beams of the ceiling were dusty racks of antlers, canteens, ropes, bridles, leather horse collars, buffalo fur gloves, lamps, saddles, packs, and pottery in rope nets. The glass counter along the other wall held a collection of seashells, tortoise shells, stone arrowheads, tins of tobacco, and pocketknives.

A few Indian women fingered the blankets on the shelf. In the corner, by the brass spittoon, a potbellied stove gave off heat and the odor of burning juniper. Several tough-looking men lounged on the wooden benches there. A dark-faced woman with steel gray hair hunched over the counter, working on a sheet of figures, and glowering each time one of the men missed the spittoon. Fargo guessed the woman was Reggio's bookkeeper.

"Doing some good business here," Fargo said, approaching her. She looked up at him disapprovingly.

"What do you want?" she snapped.

"Just commenting," he said.

She looked down again at the accounting sheet and continued her work, glancing up from time to time to shake her head at the mangy group near the stove.

Out on the plains, every newspaper that came to hand was at least a week old and usually all the good parts had been torn out by somebody who had read it before. Besides, the papers usually didn't carry news of the local happenings out in the wilds. So, the trading posts became the place that people could be sure of catching up with all the gossip.

Two of the men were now engaged in a spitting contest, edging the spittoon further away each time. Most of the time they missed entirely.

"Uncouth crowd you got here, m'am," Fargo said.

"The worst," she said, glancing up at him and giving him a tight smile.

Fargo introduced himself and found out her name was Olive Parson.

"Every year those buffalo hunters get dirtier," Olive commented, looking again at the group by the stove. "No manners." She shuddered.

"Guess it comes with the territory," Fargo said.

"Not all of the hunters are so rough," she said. "There's one of them that has fine manners. Like you. His name's Duke Manning. Big man. Handsome. And very well behaved."

Fargo remembered Yellow Dog mentioning the name of Manning as a buffalo hunter who had been in the area for a long time. He heard the note of approval in Olive Parson's voice. She must be sweet on Manning, he thought.

"Are you . . . married?" she asked, glancing down at her work. A slow blush began to light her cheeks. Fargo grinned. Olive was looking around, no doubt about it.

"I'm not the marrying kind," he said.

"Too bad," she said. "You seem like a real gentleman, and I just might know the right girl for you. If you were the settling type, that is." Olive Parson gave him another of her smiles.

Fargo allowed again that he wasn't and beat a hasty retreat out the door.

Reggio was over by the corral with the crowd of men, trading horses. Fargo walked over and took a place by the rail fence.

"That Cayuse!" Reggio sputtered. "No breeding in that mare and she's calf-kneed and bug-eyed to boot! Look, she's cribbing my corral. That's a damn bad sign." The horse was gnawing on the top rail while sucking in air. "Why she's glass-eyed and head shy! One pound of tobacco is all I'll go."

The blanket-wrapped Indian stuck out his lower lip and looked again at his claybank mare standing in the corral. The price of a good horse was three pounds of tobacco. And this was not a good horse. The Indian nodded slowly. The deal was accepted. Reggio gestured for the stable boy to take the Indian inside for the tobacco.

A black-pointed chestnut filly was led in. It cantered in long loping strides around and around the corral. Yellow Dog looked up in interest. Reggio noticed, and they began haggling in Algonquian.

"Seven buffalo robes is the highest price I pay," Yellow Dog said stubbornly, after a while. He cut the air with his hand flat, palm toward the ground to indicate he would go no higher.

"Highway robbery!" Reggio interjected in English. "Add five eagle feathers and you got yourself a pretty filly," he added in the brave's tongue.

Yellow Dog threw up his hands. "Fifteen eagle feathers buys a good horse. Seven robes," he said again, punching the air. "No more."

Reggio turned around and surveyed the crowd of men.

"Does anyone want to offer more than that for this yearling? She's a beaut."

Fargo turned away and walked down to the river to inspect the flatboat. It was the one that had been found ambushed. He walked out onto the flimsy dock and jumped onto the wooden barge. The bullet holes along the side had been made with rifles, he saw. Sharps, probably. And at close range. Very close range. He nodded to himself thoughtfully and made his way back up the hill.

Rather than walking back to the corral and the front of the trading post, Fargo angled around toward the back. Soon, the voices of the horse trading grew dim. Behind the trading post was a tall fence of new lumber which enclosed a large area to the rear of the main building. The fence went on for some distance. There was no gate to be seen. Fargo wondered what was inside. He looked for a knothole or a chink between the boards, but the fence was double-boarded, and no matter how hard he searched, he could not find a way to look inside. Lumber was a scarce commodity on the plains. The high double fence would have cost a lot to build.

He had just been about to turn back to the corral when he heard a voice. A young female voice, started to sing softly on the other side of the fence. It was a sad tune, mournful and lonely. Reggio had said there were only three of them left at the trading post—himself, the stable boy, and the bookkeeper, Olive Parsons. This was not Olive's voice.

Fargo stopped and looked up. It was too high to get over the top to look inside.

"Hello?" he called out. "Who are you?"

The voice stopped immediately, and Fargo heard a flurry of movement inside and then silence. He called out again, but there was no answer. Fargo looked about again at the rectangle of high fence. At either end, the fence joined the trading post building and was built halfway up the roofline. A barrel stood beside the building. Fargo jumped onto it and seized the roof overhang, pulling himself up easily with his powerful arms. He tried not to make too much noise as he scrambled onto the pitched roof and scurried up a few feet to look over the top of the wooden barrier.

Below was a yard. On one side a few ragged plants flowered. Three wooden chairs stood under a young cottonwood tree, and on one of them lay a square of white fabric stretched by an embroidery hoop. A sewing basket rested on the ground. A wooden door leading into the post squeaked, and Fargo ducked.

He rose again after a moment to see a willowy young woman in a pale blue dress walk hesitantly into the yard, peering anxiously around her. Gaining confidence, she seated herself on the chair, her back to Fargo, and took up her sewing. She did not sing again. Fargo raised up a little further and studied her from behind. She was young, her long neck white and bent over her work, her pale golden hair pulled back in a pink ribbon and cascading down her back.

Who was she? Fargo had never heard of a young girl living at the trading post before. He was wondering whether to call out to her when the door creaked, and he ducked again.

Reggio entered, hobbling across the yard.

Fargo braced himself on the sloping roof and peered over the fence.

The girl looked up as Reggio drew near and sat down beside her.

"I've just made some good trades," Reggio said, keeping his voice low. "More money."

The girl continued sewing and did not answer.

"A whole lot of money," Reggio added.

"I'm tired of hearing about the money!" she said. "When can I leave here?" Fargo heard the bitterness in her voice. She threw down her hoop and stood angrily.

"Gina!" Reggio said, rising and putting his arms around her. "You can't leave. You have to stay here with me. Always."

The girl burst into tears.

Fargo gritted his teeth. So, Reggio was holding the young girl captive! He felt his hand twitch over his Colt as he grasped the fence with his other hand. His eyes flicked across the roofline, planning a route to descend. When he got his hands on that hunchback . . . Fargo rose and took one step forward.

3

Fargo, balancing himself on the roof, was about to shout to Reggio to let go of the girl when she said, "Please, Father. Please, let me out of here. At least let me come into the trading post."

Fargo froze. Reggio her father? This put a different light on things. He stepped back over the part of the fence that angled across the pitched roof, and crouched behind it again. His thoughts whirled as he watched the two figures in the yard below.

"You don't understand, Gina," Reggio said, stroking her hair. "Ever since your mother died, I have tried to do what is best for you. The convent school was best for you until you came of age. Now, I am keeping you away from all those buffalo hunters. There's no telling what would happen if they got a look at you."

Fargo thought of the men he had seen inside. Reggio had a point.

"I'd be all right, Father," she said. "I could help out at the post. I could help Olive. And you'd protect me."

Reggio smiled at her.

"An old hunchback can't protect you," Reggio said. "And now the help's been scared off by those ambushes. No. You are safe here until I can save enough money to take us to town, away from here. Another couple of months. Losing those two payments on the barges set us back. But, we'll make it soon. I promise."

Gina nodded slowly.

"I try to be patient," she said. "It's just that I want so much to meet . . . a . . . a wonderful man." Gina pulled away from her father and walked across the yard, her head bent low. Fargo strained to hear the words she spoke. "Olive says I should look for a man with good manners. A tall, dark, handsome man, a powerful man. A man who would lead others . . ." Fargo smiled to himself. So, that's what Olive had been thinking when she had asked if Fargo was the marrying kind.

Reggio limped after her.

"Gina! Where did you get those crazy ideas! Answer me! Have you been talking to any men?"

"No!" she said, stooping to pick up her embroidery. "I heard a man's voice call out just before you came in, but I ran inside, just like you told me to."

In her voice Fargo heard the longing and loneliness. What a horrible life to be shut up inside the fenced yard. Even if it was temporary and for her own protection. Fargo wondered if Reggio was doing the right thing. Well, it was none of his business how the trader raised his daughter, he told himself.

"Another question," Reggio said. "Did you tell Olive about that man who was going to bring the money overland from Dodge City for me?"

Fargo remembered his conversation with Reggio. So, the old trader had confided in his daughter.

Gina was the person who couldn't have told anyone else.

"I didn't! I didn't tell Olive!"

"I'm sorry I had to ask," Reggio said. Fargo watched as Reggio embraced his daughter again. Even from a distance, Fargo could see the misery that twisted her pretty face. The hunchback left the yard. Fargo watched as Gina seated herself on the chair and tried to concentrate on her needlework. After a few moments, she threw it down again and paced back and forth along the fence, faster and faster. Finally, she burst into tears, hiding her hands in her face.

Fargo wondered if he should jump down and have a talk with her. But what good would that do? The girl was so lonely she would fall in love with the first man she met. And fall hard. That would make for some sticky complications.

Reggio was making a mistake with his daughter. That was for certain. But it wouldn't pay to interfere. And telling Reggio to let his daughter out of her confinement would only make Reggio suspect his intentions.

Silently, Fargo backed away and let himself down from the roof, landing softly on his toes on the ground outside the fence. He followed the line of the building around to the corner.

Fargo looked out across the wide dusty yard in front of the trading post. He didn't want Reggio to see him coming from behind the building and suspect he'd heard their conversation.

Three slat-bottom road wagons, piled high with buffalo robes and drawn by oxen, were just pulling up in the front of the trading post, along with a dozen men on horseback. Reggio hurried out of

49

the front door, his attention on the party which had just arrived. Fargo slipped from behind the building and walked forward nonchalantly. He watched as the buffalo hunters dismounted.

Fargo noticed one in particular, a gigantic bear of a man who must have been close to seven feet tall, with powerful broad shoulders and thick muscular arms and legs. He wore fringed buckskins and a thick brown fur cap partly shading his face. The man had turned and was barking orders to his men, who scurried about to do his bidding.

Then the big man sighted Reggio and swept the cap off his head. His face was striking with jet black curly hair and a clean-shaven chiseled jaw.

Reggio hobbled forward, his short arms swinging at his sides and a broad smile on his face.

A trading post flourished or failed based on its good relationships with the buffalo hunters and the Indians who brought in the skins and goods for trade downstream, and who bought supplies. If Reggio wanted business, he had to stay on everybody's good side.

"Duke! Duke!" the trader called excitedly. "Glad to see you back here."

So, this was Duke Manning and his bunch, Fargo thought as he watched the tall buffalo hunter stoop to extend his meaty hand toward the hunchback.

"How are you now, Mr. Reggio?" said Duke Manning. "And how's business?"

"Never better," Reggio said. "Never better."

Fargo saw a knowing look pass between the two men and Reggio patted his chest, a wide grin on his face. Duke's face darkened.

"Well now, I'm glad to hear that, Mr. Reggio,"

Duke said. He sounded anything but happy. Manning turned away from Reggio and then noticed Fargo.

"Who's this?" Duke asked. Fargo felt Duke's hard eyes on him, and he returned the gaze.

"You ever heard of the Trailsman?" Reggio said. "Well, this is him."

Manning's deep-set eyes glittered with interest. And something else.

"Really?" he said. "So, this is this famous Trailsman. Got quite a reputation, Mr. Trailsman." Manning's dark eyes examined him head to toe, taking in Fargo's long muscular frame.

"Name's Skye Fargo." He reached out to shake the buffalo hunter's hand.

"Duke Manning."

Manning's grip was like iron. And as he seized Fargo's hand, he gripped harder. Fargo clenched his jaw and returned the pressure, his face unmoving. For a long moment, they held the grip, eyes locked. He'd hate to come up against Manning hand to hand, Fargo thought. The man was built like a gigantic ox.

"Glad to know you," Manning said, releasing his hand. "What brings you out here, Mr. Fargo?"

Manning had an annoying habit of calling everyone Mister.

"Making some deliveries to Fort McKinney. The Gilded Cage. And here."

Manning shot a look at Reggio, who smiled and patted his chest again.

"Is that so?" Duke asked thoughtfully. "You making a delivery to Reggio's Trading Post. Well, how lucky for Mr. Reggio that you happened along. Is that what the Trailsman does for a living? Makes deliveries?" Manning paused and flashed his white smile at Fargo, but his eyes were humorless and brooding. "You one of those men who can be hired out to do odd jobs?"

Fargo clenched his fists. Manning was baiting him now. Trying to see what would get under his skin. Trying to see where his temper would boil. But why?

"I take on jobs other men can't do," Fargo said, keeping his voice cold. "I like the challenge." Fargo smiled very slowly at the hunter. "It's a helluva lot better than sitting on the prairie and mowing down a bunch of helpless buffalo, for instance."

Manning's dark eyes spit black fire. He'd hit a nerve for sure, Fargo thought as he watched the huge man's jaw ripple as he ground his teeth together.

"Ahem!" Reggio broke in nervously. "Duke, why don't you show me what you've got? We could use some good quality robes like you had last time. The ones so well tanned. I'm sending a shipment downstream in a few more days."

Manning turned away from Fargo as if he'd forgotten he was there and led Reggio over to one of the wagons. Fargo headed toward the corral, passing close to one of Manning's wagons on the way. He paused to examine the tower of skins piled inside.

Many of the robes had been stripped from the bison, staked and let dry until they were as hard as flint. These skins still needed to be treated and finished before they could be sold again downriver. Another pile of the skins had been tanned. Fargo reached out to bury his hand in the deep, rough fur. Skins taken from the buffalo in the fall and winter, when the fur was thickest, sold for the highest prices. He pulled back a corner of the robe and examined the skin. Damn good job of tanning, he thought.

Usually, the white hunters didn't wait around to scrape and soften skins. It was time consuming. They generally preferred to spend their time killing and left the long tanning process to somebody else, even though the untanned ones sold for less.

Fargo turned away from Manning's wagon and continued on to the corral where he found Yellow Dog.

"Old friend of the Cheyenne," Yellow Dog said, nodding toward Duke Manning. "Many times he is welcomed in our village. Many times he makes us gifts."

Fargo nodded, not enthusiastically. He didn't like Duke Manning the first instant he met him. And it was hard to say just why. A man that size could be a real bully. Outwardly, Manning was courteous. But Manning's handshake was the mark of a man who not only wanted to lead, but to rule and dominate.

Fargo watched as Reggio hopped from wagon to wagon, examining the furs, gesticulating and bargaining with Manning. They were an unlikely pair, the giant and the hunchback.

Fargo noticed that Yellow Dog was looking at him carefully.

"You do not like Manning," the brave observed.

"No," Fargo admitted.

"He is a strong man. Almost like a spirit god. And a great hunter," Yellow Dog said. "He has hunted on these plains for a long time and he knows the buffalo. Not like other white men."

Fargo nodded again, watching as Manning laughed and slapped Reggio so hard on the back that the little man nearly toppled over and barely managed to steady himself.

"Many white hunters, they take only the robe and the tongue of the buffalo. But Duke Manning sends his men to tell us where he has killed, and he makes gifts of the meat." Yellow Dog said. "Other white hunters bring the soft men from the East to hunt buffalo. The soft men have much gold. And they are stupid. They make noise and shoot their guns before they are ready. Then the buffalo run. But Manning does not bring these soft men to hunt. He continues to hunt in the old way."

Yellow Dog was laying it on thick, Fargo thought. Maybe he'd misjudged Duke Manning. After all, if the Cheyenne had known Manning for years and accepted him . . . But the thought didn't change Fargo's mind about the buffalo hunter.

Reggio and Manning were nodding, having come to some kind of agreement about the goods in the wagons. Olive Parson stepped out of the post and sighted Duke Manning. She hurried forward, patting down her graying hair.

"Oh! Mr. Manning! You're here!"

"Well, if it isn't Madam Parson!" Manning said. He bowed gallantly and kissed Olive Parson's hand. They conversed for a moment. Fargo noted that Olive Parson was gazing up in rapt attention at the giant man while she dug holes in the dust with the pointed toe of her laced boot. Finally, she excused herself and clanged an iron triangle hung near the door. Fargo noticed he was hungry, and he and Yellow Dog headed inside.

The grub was cheap, plentiful, and good. Fargo loaded more beans and beef on his plate and headed back to a seat beside Yellow Dog at the long wooden table. Reggio and Manning disappeared down the hallway which led to the office.

As soon as Manning left the room, his men became louder and more boisterous. Manning's crew was a ragged bunch, none as distinguished as Manning himself. Most wore tattered skins and grimy slouch hats.

Fargo turned to look at the grizzled young man sitting next to him. In his dark, sun-lined face, Fargo saw the wary, darting gaze of a frontier man who scraped a living any way he could manage. A buffalo hunting crew did a lot of dirty work.

The actual shooting of the bison took only a few minutes. The crew spent most of their day skinning the beasts out in the hot sun amid pools of blood and swarms of flies. It wasn't a job for weak men.

"How's the hunting season?" Fargo asked.

"Fair," the man answered. A long silence followed.

"I ran into a buffalo hunter in Fort McKinney," Fargo said, keeping his voice conversational. "We had a real nice exchange in a bar. Maybe you know him. He has a big brown beard and brown eyes. About your height and kind of stocky. Curly hair."

The young man's eyes narrowed.

"There's a lot of buffalo hunters fit that description," the man said. He picked up his plate and moved several seats away. Well, the only thing he had learned was that the young man didn't want to talk. That could mean something. Or nothing.

Fargo wondered again who had sent the brown-bearded man to shoot him and why. Could it have been Manning? Was it connected with the money he was carrying for Reggio? Or was it something else altogether?

When they had finished eating, the hunters piled their plates onto the sideboard and swept the table clean. All gathered around. Wads of money and stacks of coins appeared. One pulled out a piece of chalk and made some marks on the wooden table. Another man drew dice from his pocket and threw them, clattering, across the tabletop.

"Manning's crew likes to gamble," Yellow Dog said, glancing toward the tables longingly. He opened his parfleche and removed a handful of silver coins, gazed down at them, and then looked again at the table where the men had already laid down their first bets. He joined the crowd, and Fargo followed.

"Put your bets down now," a baldheaded man said. Yellow Dog threw a couple of the coins onto a chalk square marked with the number seven. Other piles of money were on the rest of the numbers. No one bet on nine. The baldheaded man rolled. The dice came up nine and he raked the money across the table toward himself.

"Lay 'em down," he said.

Fargo watched for a few more rounds, as Yellow Dog continued to lay his coins down on the squares and lose, time after time. Two other Indians, Cheyenne from other bands, had joined in along with three riverboat men. They were losing, too, and, one by one, they withdrew from the game as Yellow Dog continued to play, winning a little and losing even more.

The only men who consistently won money were in Manning's outfit. Mostly, the dice came up with the number no one bet, often nine or two. Fargo was dead certain the dice were loaded and he watched the man with the dice closely. Each time he got ready to roll, he rolled the dice in his palms, sometimes stopping to scratch himself under one arm. Fargo saw his fingers slip inside his pocket. He had several pairs of dice. And he was switching off. He threw again.

When the dice came up nine again, landing right in front of him, Fargo swept them up in his hand.

"What the hell?" the bald man exclaimed. "Give me those dice!"

Fargo held them on the palm of his hand and examined them closely. They'd been shaved, sure enough, the corners rounded to make the dice more likely to land on one number rather than another. He rolled them in his palm, feeling their unevenness. They'd been weighted, too.

Fargo shot a look at the bald man, a look he well understood, for he rose half in his chair, his hand reaching slowly for his side arm. In a flash, Fargo drew the Colt and covered him.

"Freeze!" Fargo said. The man didn't move. Fargo smiled very slowly.

"One more bet," he said. "And I'll roll." Manning's men muttered to themselves, but nobody drew. Fargo suspected they were all in on the crooked dice.

Fargo reached across the table and raked the stack of the bald man's earnings onto the number six.

"Hey, wait a minute," the man said.

"Put all of yours on nine," Fargo said to Yellow Dog.

"You men put what you've got left on nine, too," Fargo said to the couple of Indians and riverboat men, who were now only watching the game. They hesitantly put some of their remaining money on nine.

Fargo rolled and the dice skittered across the table, coming up four and five. The winners cheered and divided the pile of bills and coins among them.

"Take your money and get out of here," Fargo said to Yellow Dog. "Wait for me over the second rise. I'll be along soon." He still held his Colt in front of him. A red flush of anger was creeping across the bald man's face. The rest of Manning's crew were rumbling. Trouble could break out at any moment.

The Indians and the riverboat men backed out of the door. Fargo waited until they were clear and he heard the sound of their hoofbeats die away. Then he slowly holstered his gun.

He stood where he was, defiant. The bald man threw angry looks at him, but didn't go for his pistol again. Instead, he pulled a deck of cards and began to deal. The men shifted on their feet and then slowly pulled money from their pockets, ignoring Fargo.

Fargo backed toward Reggio's office. Manning's

men watched him sullenly, but no one made a move. He'd made a lot of enemies tonight, Fargo thought. Well, with luck, he wouldn't run into Manning's men again soon.

After he had a brief word with the trader, he'd meet Yellow Dog and ride with him until he was sure they weren't being followed. Then they'd camp for the night. In the morning, he'd return to The Gilded Cage.

Fargo walked down a short corridor out of sight of the angry hunters. Behind the door, he heard Reggio and Manning talking. Just as he was about to knock, he paused.

"Yes, I've got the money I owe you," Reggio's voice was saying, "but I want that note back."

"What note?" Manning asked casually.

"You know damn well what note," Reggio said. "The one that gives you title to this trading post if I don't pay up."

So, that was why Reggio was so desperate to get the money delivered safely. And why he had been so relieved when Fargo had arrived. His whole operation had been at stake.

"Oh, that note. I don't have it with me. But don't worry, Mr. Reggio," Manning's voice was smooth and soothing. "We've been trading partners for a long time now. We've always trusted one another. Give me the money you owe, and as soon as I find that note, I'll hand it over to you."

"Sorry, Manning. No note, no cash," Reggio said.

"What?" Manning said. "You want to keep doing business with me and my boys, don't you? Then give me that money. Surely you trust me. And you know damn well what I can do to this place. A word from me, and nobody will trade here. Now, give me that money . . ."

This was as good a time as any. Fargo knocked, his hand over his Colt. There was a sudden silence inside the room.

"Who is it?" Reggio's voice called.

Fargo identified himself, and Reggio let him inside.

Manning sat at a table in a pool of golden light from the oil lamp. Two glasses stood between the two chairs, along with a whiskey bottle, nearly empty.

"What do you want?" Reggio asked. He was acting as though nothing was the matter.

"You got some trouble in here?" Fargo asked, darting a look at Manning.

Reggio laughed nervously.

"Well, maybe you overheard us having some heated words just now," the hunchback said. "Let me assure you, Duke Manning is one of my best customers. We're just enjoying a little friendly bartering. Nothing out of the ordinary." Reggio laughed again. Manning smiled.

Well, if Reggio didn't want his help, he certainly couldn't force it on him, Fargo thought. Still, he didn't like what he had overheard. Reggio was a shrewd trader. And he owed Manning money. But Fargo was almost certain that Manning meant to double-cross Reggio, probably by holding on to that note of ownership of the trading post. But Reggio could take care of himself. Fargo gave Manning another glance and then made up his mind.

"Well then, I'm heading out," Fargo said.

"I'm much obliged for what you did, Skye,"

Reggio said. "I might need to call on you again sometime."

"Suits me fine," Fargo said. "One more thing. Do you get any Kiowa trading here?" Duke Manning shifted in his chair.

"Kiowa? They usually stay south of the Arkansas," Reggio said. "That's their territory. But every month or so, a party of them comes up this way."

"When did the Kiowa come through last?"

Reggio scratched his head for a moment.

"Hmm. Now that I think of it, it's been quite a while. They're overdue here, I guess. That's strange."

"You might have some Indian trouble brewing," Fargo said. "On the way into Fort McKinney, I found a Cheyenne brave killed with a Kiowa hatchet in him. And Yellow Dog told me it wasn't the first he'd seen."

"Oh hell," Reggio said. He paced back and forth a moment, dragging one foot behind him. "If the Cheyenne and Kiowa start fighting . . . well, everything will be all right for a while. But the army won't cotton to a bunch of armed Indians on the warpath. Some stupid foot soldier or a nervous settler will start shooting and then . . ."

"Exactly," Fargo said.

"Last time there were Indian wars," Reggio said, "the army killed about a third of the Indians here. God, it was bloody. But there's a lot more army here now. This time, it would be even worse. On Indians and whites."

"I wouldn't worry about the Indians. Redskins can take care of themselves," Manning said, pouring the last of the whiskey into his glass. "I should know. I practically live with them. If they want to have a war, I say we whites ought to stay the hell out of it."

"What do you think about these killings?" Fargo asked the buffalo hunter.

Manning downed the drink.

"First I've heard of it," he said a little too loudly. "Doesn't make sense to me. But then, the Indians are just savages. A white man's gotta keep that in mind all the time. They look like men, and sometimes they act like men. And if you treat them right, you get along fine. You scatter around a few trinkets, and they're happy. Pay the price, and they leave you alone. You learn what's important to them, and they like you fine. But keep in mind they're just savages. Every damn one of them."

"I'll keep your opinions in mind," Fargo said. Manning was as two-faced as they came, Fargo thought. Friend of the Indians, indeed.

"Oh, another thing, Mr. Trailsman," Manning said. "I might want to hire you sometime for some odd jobs of my own. I'm sure you're always looking for work."

"Not really," Fargo said, feeling his blood run hot. Manning had a way of getting under a man's skin. "I only take jobs that suit me. I doubt working for you would."

"I'll walk you out," Reggio said, taking Fargo's arm and pulling him toward the door. Fargo went along with the trader. There was nothing to be gained by trading more verbal insults with Duke Manning.

They passed by the gambling table on their way out. Reggio paused. Several of the men looked up at Fargo with narrowed eyes.

"Reggio!" the bald man called out across the room. "How about a game?"

"I wouldn't play if I were you," Fargo said quietly to Reggio. "The dice are loaded."

"Loaded! That's ridiculous!" Reggio said. "I've played many times before with these men. I've known them for a long time. Duke wouldn't put up with loaded dice. Besides, I'm feeling lucky tonight."

"Suit yourself," Fargo said.

Reggio limped toward the table, drawing a roll of bills from his pocket. It looked like the same money Fargo had delivered earlier. He threw some of the bills down and waited for the roll. He won and collected his pile, shooting a triumphant look at Fargo over his shoulder as he put all his winnings back down on the table and added a few more bills from his wad. He won again, and he laughed, shaking his head from side to side. Someone poured him a whiskey and slid it across the table.

Fargo made his way to the front door and turned to look back. Reggio had tossed another pile of money down and was concentrating on the roll of the dice. All the men were leaning forward around the table.

Fargo thought of Gina, kept hidden in the back of the trading post until Reggio could make enough money to take her away to town. This wasn't the way to do it, Fargo thought.

On the other side of the room, Fargo saw Duke Manning emerge from the corridor. The big man leaned against a doorjamb watching the game, a small smile on his face. He noticed Fargo's gaze and nodded to him, his face expressionless.

There was nothing further he could do here. Fargo turned and walked out into the early dusk.

They were five miles out from the post and the pale blue sky still held light when the Ovaro whinnied nervously. Fargo scanned the darkening land until he saw a dark lump some half mile away on the prairie. He pointed it out to Yellow Dog, who was leading a string of packhorses, one dragging a travois. The brave nodded, and Fargo galloped toward it.

The Kiowa warrior was facedown in the earth. His Appaloosa lay nearby. The vultures had done their work on both corpses. It had been a day or two since the killing, and the smell was high. Fargo tied his bandana around his face and dismounted to get a closer look. The Ovaro trotted a short distance away, not liking the smell of death.

Fargo leaned over and pulled the Cheyenne arrow from the brave's shoulder. It came loose easily. The back of the skull had been shattered, but there wasn't enough flesh left to tell whether it had been a bullet or a club that had killed the man. Fargo turned and walked into the wind for a hundred paces to get clear of the odor, then drew deep draughts of fresh air into his lungs.

Yellow Dog came up, leading his string.

"Kiowa," Fargo said. He held up the Cheyenne arrow.

"Good," Yellow Dog said. He did not stop, but continued riding, the travois scraping two deep troughs through the earth after him.

Fargo whistled to the pinto, which came at once. He mounted and followed.

It wasn't good, he thought. Not one goddamn thing about it was good.

4

An hour later, they camped by the creek in a hollow that would shield the light of their small campfire. The coyotes were close, their howls and yips coming from just over the next rise. The waxing moon was high and the autumn air chilly when they turned in. Fargo threw an extra blanket over his bedroll, and Yellow Dog bundled himself into a buffalo robe.

The next morning, Fargo rose before the sun and brewed the coffee while Yellow Dog fed their horses. In half an hour, they were saddled and ready to part company. They had hardly spoken to one another the evening before or that morning. Fargo's thoughts had been occupied with what he had seen at the trading post, as well as with concerns about the Indian war which seemed to be imminent. It had been clear from Yellow Dog's reaction to the dead Kiowa that he was ready to fight. Clearly, some of the Cheyenne were already taking retribution for their own murdered braves.

But there was something about it all that didn't add up. It wasn't like the Cheyenne, or the Kiowa, to murder members of another tribe riding alone on the plains with no provocation. Especially when there was a treaty in effect.

Fargo prepared to mount and then thought of the pieces of carved bone in his pocket. The ones he had found on the dead man. He called Yellow Dog over and withdrew them from his pocket.

The brave bent over to look at them closely and then straightened. He shrugged.

"Cheyenne," he said. "A game of gambling. I hold the pieces in my fists. You guess which one is where. Then we bet money. It is an old game with us."

"The man who tried to kill me yesterday had these in his pocket," Fargo said.

Yellow Dog shrugged again.

"Many men are gamblers," he said and turned away toward his horse.

Fargo pocketed the pieces of bone again. Unfortunately, they proved nothing conclusive. But they suggested that the brown-bearded man had liked gambling. And, he'd been familiar enough with the Cheyenne to learn their games. Fargo's thoughts went immediately to Duke Manning and his crew. It certainly fit, didn't it? But there were too many questions still unanswered. It wasn't enough to go on. Not yet.

Fargo and the brave mounted. Yellow Dog was heading north toward the Cheyenne camp and Fargo due west back to McKinney and The Gilded Cage.

"Please give a message to Broken Bow," Fargo said. The Indian nodded. "Tell him not to go to war until I come to talk to him. Tell him to wait as long as possible before fighting. I will come to talk." The words were out of his mouth before he knew he was going to say them. And when he heard them spoken, he realized that he didn't know exactly what he would say to Broken Bow. But by talking to the Cheyenne, he hoped he could get to the bottom of why the tribes were killing each other.

Yellow Dog nodded slowly.

"I will give the message to my father." His eyes were angry. "And it is a message he will want to hear. He is an old man, and his fight is gone. But I say the Kiowa kill us. We kill them. They are not to be trusted now. They have broken the treaty. Not us."

"What about the dead Kiowa last night?" Fargo asked. "That was a Cheyenne arrow in his shoulder. If a Cheyenne killed that brave, then Cheyenne have broken the treaty, too."

"It was only right," Yellow Dog said. "Kiowa killed first. And I do not want peace. I am sick of peace. We are warriors. Warriors must fight."

Fargo shook his head sadly and said goodbye. The Ovaro leapt forward, his gleaming white-and-black markings glistening in the morning sunlight.

He had ridden another hour when he felt the pinto pause in its stride, head up, nostrils flaring in the wind. Fargo gazed across the sea of empty yellow grasses. He loosened the Sharps rifle in its saddle holster, then moved forward warily.

A mile on, he paused at the top of a long rise and looked down at the fresh kill. The raw, bloody corpses of more than thirty buffalo littered the grass. All but one had been stripped of their woolly coats and tongues. The rest of the meat would be left to rot.

A team of five men was struggling to load the

heavy wet robes, sodden with blood, onto a wagon. Fargo watched as the skinner bent to slit the hide from the last unskinned buffalo. He slid his long knife from the head down between the legs, then cut around each leg and loosened the skin around the neck. Another man approached, leading a balking horse. They attached a rope through a slit in the hide, and the horse moved forward slowly, peeling the skin off by slow degrees as several of them shifted the mammoth body.

Three other men sat on horseback watching the skinning. One noticed him and waved. Fargo approached.

"Hail, stranger!" one called out as he drew near. The man was dressed in extravagantly fringed and beaded buckskins, spanking new. His slouch hat was spotless as well. There was a flush of red sunburn on his pale neck.

Eastern dandy, Fargo knew. Out for the great adventure to hunt buffalo in the Wild West.

"I'm Louis Vandermeer and this is Mortimer Frank." The man gestured toward a man astride a dappled gray.

The second dandy wore ridiculously wide chaps which stuck out like wings. Hell, there was no chaparral around for a few hundred miles, Fargo thought. He noted the dandy's long roweled spurs the size of flapjacks and winced at the horse's sides, which were mangled as ground beef.

The third man was clearly the leader of the buffalo hunting crew below. Under a gray shock of hair, his bronzed face was deeply lined and his clothes were tattered and stained. Fargo ignored the other two and nodded to the third.

"I've run across some dead braves," Fargo said without preamble. "Cheyenne killed by Kiowa and vice versa. You seen any of that?"

The two dandies exchanged glances and shook their heads vehemently. The buffalo hunter spat a long stream of yellow tobacco before he spoke.

"Yep. Ran across two Kiowa and one Cheyenne in the last four days," the old man said.

"What?" the man in buckskins said. "We haven't seen anything of the sort!"

"Found 'em the last three mornings while you boys were still sleeping," the old man said unsmilingly. "Ain't a good sign."

Fargo nodded and looked off toward the horizon.

"Does that mean the redskins are on the warpath?" Mortimer Frank asked nervously. He glanced up at the horizon as though he expected to see a thousand screaming Indians racing toward him.

"How's the hunting?" Fargo asked.

"Well, today we got more than thirty of them!" Vandermeer answered. "It's the best day we've had so far . . ." Fargo ignored him pointedly, and he fell silent.

"Not a bad season," the old man said slowly. "Buffalo are running late this year and moving slow. We'll have a mild winter in these parts."

"Where do you sell?" Fargo asked.

"Over at Reggio's," the old hunter said. "You know him?"

Fargo nodded. The two easterners continued to listen, their eyes wide.

"Real bastard," the old man said bitterly. "Gives this Duke Manning the best prices. You know him, too?"

"Yeah," Fargo said. "And I don't like him either."

"Well, there are goddamn few of us," the old man said. "Manning's popular around here. Can't figure out why. He's got Reggio under his thumb. And now he's got a tight rein on most of the independent buffalo runners around here. He skims their profits, takes robes off them if he wants to."

"In exchange for what?" Fargo asked.

"Protection," the old man said with a bitter laugh. "Protection from one of his men creeping up on you in the middle of the night, most likely. Most buffalo runners just figure it's some kind of tax. But I say to hell with it. I ain't giving Manning none of my robes. He's caught up with me a few times. But mostly I bring my robes into Reggio's in the middle of the night when I know Manning and his gang aren't there. Duke'll catch up with me someday, once and for all. But until then, I say to hell with him!"

"Between Manning and these Indian killings, you'd better keep your eyes open."

"Always have," the old man said. "Be seeing you."

As Fargo's pinto took off, the two dandies shouted for him to come back and talk to them, but he was already galloping away, not eager to be part of the show.

The wagon, piled high with bloody robes, tongues, and two buffalo heads was creaking up the slope, followed by the team on horseback. Fargo galloped by them, then through the scattered bodies. There were hundreds of men on the plains, each of them killing thirty, sixty, ninety buffalo a day, and sending the robes back east. There were millions upon millions of the bison on the great plains, so many that sometimes a herd took more than a day to pass by, stretching from horizon to horizon. Still, the naked bloodied carcasses of the buffalo lying on the plain bothered Fargo. It was a waste of the animal. He rode on.

"Duke Manning?" Sylvia exclaimed, throwing her hands in the air. "Oh, that man! Don't get me started." She shook her head and then smiled across the table at Fargo while she played with one of the blond ringlets which lay on her bare shoulder. "I don't want to talk about Duke Manning when we were having such a pleasant time."

"It's a wonderful steak," Fargo said. She had had the meal sent up to her room when he arrived.

"And after a leisurely dinner, we'll have a leisurely bath." She smiled and nodded toward the copper tub sitting next to her four-poster bed. "And then we'll have a leisurely . . ." She smiled again, her dimples showing. She crossed her arms and leaned against the table, her creamy white breasts pushing up over her low-cut purple dress.

"Very leisurely," Fargo said, "suits me fine."

Fargo poured her another glass of wine. The candlelight made it sparkle like rubies. Sylvia idly played with the Indian shell necklaces around her neck. They contrasted oddly with her satin dress.

"But I still want to know about Duke Manning," Fargo said. "I ran into him and his men at Reggio's."

"Duke Manning . . ." Sylvia frowned and took a sip of wine. "He's been around these parts for years hunting buffalo," she began. "But he's only been making trouble for the past couple of years."

"What kind of trouble?" Fargo asked.

Sylvia shifted uncomfortably.

"Now, I don't mean trouble exactly. I don't want to stir up anything," she said.

"What kind of trouble?" Fargo repeated.

"It's, well, subtle," Sylvia began, hesitantly. "I guess it was a few years ago when Duke and his boys started showing up here at The Gilded Cage regularly. Before that, we didn't see much of them." She took a sip of wine and looked about, as if afraid someone would overhear. "And, you know, Duke's got all the other buffalo hunters under his control."

"I heard that," said Fargo. "So?"

"So, he's been . . . well, it's hard to explain."

"Look, Sylvia," Fargo said. "You've never been one to mince words. What's going on with Manning?"

"Well, he comes in here," she said. "And, you've seen him, he's a big man. Why, he's so tall I just clear his belt buckle. He could deck anybody with one finger. And he's got his favorite girls. And his favorite drinks." She paused.

"I don't get it, Sylvia," said Fargo.

"Duke Manning always has good manners with all the girls. And everyone thinks he's so nice. But then, every once in a while he drops a hint or two." Sylvia shifted in her chair again, her cheeks reddening.

"Speak plainly, Sylvia," Fargo said. "What kind of a hint?"

She shook her head.

"I'm sorry. I know I sound strange. It's just that when I explain it to you, it sounds so stupid that I can't believe it myself. You see, Duke Manning started coming in here and saying that if things didn't please him at The Gilded Cage, he'd take his business elsewhere. But he never said that in so many words. He just hinted at it."

"You could certainly do without Duke Manning."

"Oh, sure. But then he implied that if he left, none of the other buffalo hunters would be coming here either."

"Could he keep them out of The Gilded Cage?"

"I think so," Sylvia said. "He's got some kind of control over all the hunting crews. And, those buffalo hunters are about half my business."

Fargo thought for a minute.

"So, he's got you over the barrel," he said slowly. "And what does he ask in return for his continued patronage of The Gilded Cage?"

Sylvia looked down at her plate.

"Well, at first he didn't ask for much," she said. "Every once in a while, he'd say he wasn't going to pay for a girl and that I should consider it as a cost of doing business with the buffalo hunters. Well, business was pretty good, and I could put up with that every once in a while . . ."

"And then?"

Sylvia hung her head.

"I've always been such a good businesswoman," she said. "Damn it, it's hard for me to believe this has happened to me. Duke Manning kept pressuring me to give him services for free—oh, not mine, but some of the girls'—and then it got so he wanted free drinks. And then free drinks for his men. And then, one month, when business got real bad, he got me to . . . oh hell!"

Sylvia rose suddenly from the table and crossed the room to stand in front of the window. Even from across the room, Fargo could see that she was quaking with rage.

"He got me to sign over twenty percent of my business!" she said. "Goddamn him!"

"For what?" Fargo asked.

"To keep coming here. To keep his men coming here. To keep all the buffalo hunters coming here. At first, I thought it would be worth it. After all, they're half my business and paying twenty percent to keep fifty percent is still coming out ahead. Except now, all the buffalo hunters come here and expect free hospitality. So, they're getting a free ride. *And* I'm paying Duke Manning!"

"That's extortion," Fargo said. "Did you have any witnesses when he threatened you?"

"No, damn him," she said. "He was too clever for that. And that document I signed is as legal as can be. Lots of times I've thought about telling Sheriff Smythe. Or Colonel Straver. But there's nothing they could do really. I've been stupid. And I've been taken. And there's nothing I can do to prove Duke Manning was threatening me!"

Sylvia stamped her foot and clenched her fists. Then she burst into tears.

Fargo rose and came up behind her. He put his arms around her, and she turned, burying her head against him.

"Duke . . . Manning is one reason . . . I'm closing down . . ." she said, between sobs. "Oh . . . I want to try ranching . . . Always have." She pulled a handkerchief from her waistband and dried her eyes. "This situation with Duke just made my decision a little easier. I just want to get away from Manning and his bunch."

Fargo smiled down at her and lifted her chin, leaning over to kiss her. Her lips parted, and his tongue darted into her mouth, exploring her warm sweetness. Her hands stroked his back in long caresses, gently, then more urgently.

He pulled away, kissing her forehead, and stroked her hair.

"Leave Manning to me," he said. "The bastard."

"Skye, please don't," Sylvia said stiffening. "You don't know Duke like I do. He's a dangerous man. And a strong man. I've seen the kind of trouble he can cause."

"Like sending someone to shoot me down in a crowded bar?"

Sylvia started.

"That man *was* shooting at you, wasn't he? He just happened to kill Mandy, God rest his soul. But what makes you think Manning sent him? And why you?"

"I can't prove anything yet," said Fargo slowly. "But I was carrying some money to deliver to the trading post. And Manning wanted to scare off anybody who would help Reggio get his payments. You see, Duke's been doing almost the same thing to Reggio that he's been doing to you. I'm convinced that shooting me was part of his plan to eventually gain control of the trading post."

"You'll have a hard time proving anything about Duke Manning," Sylvia said. "He's a slick one."

"I'll get him somehow," Fargo said. "If it's the last thing I do."

Sylvia shuddered.

"Don't say that," she said. "Come, let's finish eating. I knew it would spoil our dinner to talk about Duke."

Fargo let her lead him back to the table, where

they finished the bottle of wine and had dessert. Then Sylvia poured him a large snifter of brandy and rang a small silver bell. A rotund woman in a large white apron came in to clear the table and fill the copper tub full of steaming water.

When she had gone, Sylvia disappeared behind a folding screen in a corner of the room. Fargo sipped his brandy as he watched the purple dress and a parade of petticoats being tossed over the top of the screen. Finally, Sylvia stepped out from behind the screen, wrapped in a gauzy pink robe which hid almost nothing.

Through the translucent fabric, he could see the curves of her round breasts, soft pink nipples, and large areolas. His eyes lingered on her hourglass waist, rounded hips, and the golden triangle between her slender legs.

He remembered her, wanted her, felt himself hardening in anticipation that was almost an ache to be inside of her again.

She smiled and came over to him as he sat at the table. She took the glass of brandy from his grasp, lifted it to her lips, took a sip but didn't swallow and then bent over to kiss him. Her lips, as they touched his, tasted of the rich liqueur, and then her tongue slid into his mouth and the brandy poured into his mouth from hers, burning and tingling and rising through his nose and into his head as he drank in her mouth, her tongue, her lips.

As he kissed her, he moved his hands inside the robe and slowly up her small slenderness to cup her soft flesh, gently stroking the nipples as they hardened and grew erect. He pulled her down toward him, taking one breast into his mouth, rolling the hard button of flesh between his teeth, his tongue, his lips. Sylvia moaned.

"Oh, Skye. You don't know how many times I've thought of you and wished you were here with me . . . Oh."

Her hands fumbled with his shirt. Her cool fingers slipped inside to caress the muscular breadth of his chest. Then he felt her loosen his belt, and he stood as she undid his jeans. They dropped to the floor along with his drawers.

"Um," she said, her eyes on his huge hardness. "How I've missed you."

Fargo pulled her close as she dropped the robe around her. Then he lifted her in his arms.

"Bath? Or bed?"

She smiled up at him and then glanced over at the steaming tub.

"Seems a shame to waste all that hot water," she said, clasping her hands about his neck.

Fargo carried her over to the tub, and stepped in, still carrying her in his arms. He bent forward to place her into the water, but she held her hands clasped around his neck so that she hung down in front of him for a moment. Then she lifted her legs and hooked them around his waist, pulling her slender hips upward until her warm wetness suddenly nuzzled against the tip of him. He smiled down at her as she very slowly tightened her legs and he slid inside her.

"Neat trick," he said as she giggled.

He slowly lowered the two of them into the warm water as she clung to him, moving slowly back and forth. Fargo sat in the copper tub with Sylvia facing him. He leaned toward her and kissed her again, plunging his tongue into her mouth as he felt her tighten rhythmically around him, small fluttering motions deep inside her. He put his hand under the water and traced a line up her thigh to her fur, then found her hard button and stroked her gently, teasingly, as she began to pant.

"Oh, Skye. Please. Yes."

He pushed his hips forward, feeling her tighten around him again and again, back and forth. With his other hand he grasped her buttocks and pushed into her more insistently as the water began to slosh around in the tub. He continued to stroke her and felt her inner contractions increase.

"Yes, yes."

It was gathering at the base of him, urgent, unstoppable, the pleasure about to explode. He held it back until her gasps tore at her.

"Yes, Now. Oh . . . oh, God!"

And he thrust again, deep into her tightness as water sloshed out of the tub and the room exploded in colors, ecstasy, forgetfulness, again and again and again as she cried out and clung to him.

Finally, he was spent and he lay back in the tub, pulling Sylvia onto his chest as her breathing slowed.

"Oh, Skye," she said at last. "I've never met another man like you." She shivered.

"The water's getting cold," he said.

"Let's get out and dry off. Then you could warm me up."

Fargo grinned.

"Anything you say. But, I thought I was getting my reward for bringing in those petticoats."

"That's right!" Sylvia laughed. "Well then, anything *you* say . . ."

Fargo lay back on the feather pillows and closed his eyes against the morning light. He listened to Sylvia humming as she poured coffee into the two cups. There was a knock on the door, and he heard her answer it.

"Message for Mr. Fargo," a woman's voice said. Fargo opened his eyes as Sylvia approached the bed carrying a folded paper sealed with wax.

Fargo broke the seal as Sylvia brought him his coffee and set it down on the table beside the bed.

The handwriting was scrawled, clearly written in haste.

"You are my only hope," the message said. "Please come quickly or my life is ended. I will pay anything you ask. Reggio."

Fargo handed the paper to Sylvia and picked up his coffee cup, draining it as she scanned the letter. She looked up over the edge of the paper.

"Duke Manning?"

"You can bet your life on it," Fargo said, rising from the bed and reaching for his clothes.

"Oh, Skye," she said, her voice edged with worry. "I just don't want you to bet *yours*."

The pinto galloped tirelessly east across the rolling empty plain. For hours, the only change in the scenery had been the clouds marching west to east against the blue sky and the occasional pile of buffalo bones or rotting carcasses.

There was plenty of time to think, mostly about Duke Manning. There was no doubt that whatever trouble Reggio was in, Manning would be at the root of it.

Well, if he had to fight Manning—directly or indirectly—he would have to find a weak point. Every man had a fatal weakness which was sometimes disguised as a strength.

Manning was strong. Powerful. And clever. An almost invincible combination. In his mind, Fargo turned over all the small details he had observed about Manning . . . his grip, his manners, his self-confidence, his striking looks, his powerful frame and gigantic stature. Then he thought of the conversation he had had with Manning about the Indians.

They weren't even men, they were savages, Manning had said. But the Indians believed Duke was their friend. Well, that might come in handy, thought Fargo.

And there was Manning's greed. He wanted to take over Reggio's Trading Post. He wanted a cut of The Gilded Cage. A man who was that greedy would make a mistake. Would take a shortcut sometime. And Fargo would be waiting for it.

Unless Manning knew Fargo was after him and got him first.

Fargo sighted moving figures on the tawny grass, some distance ahead. He loosened the Sharps rifle and slowed the Ovaro as he narrowed his eyes and tried to make out who it was.

Soon he was close enough to make out the hunters he had met up with the day before—the two eastern dandies and the old hunter. Several buffalo calves lay on the ground. The hunters had clearly run them down on horseback and were waiting for the crew of skinners and wagoners to catch up. Fargo saw the wagons come over the horizon several miles away as he headed toward them.

And then he saw something else. A lone Indian suddenly appeared on a rise as if he sprang out of the earth itself. A scout, Fargo knew. Traveling alone in advance of the main body.

The Indian sat on horseback as still as a rock. He had sighted Fargo as well as the buffalo hunters. Finally, the brave started toward them slowly. The Indian would reach the hunters at about the same time that Fargo did. Even at this distance, he could recognize the distinctive yellow Kiowa war shield.

The dandies tried to pull out their rifles when they sighted the Indian approaching, but put them up when the old buffalo hunter told them to with an impatient gesture of his hand.

Fargo rode up as the Kiowa brave came to a halt before the three hunters.

"You are far from home," Fargo said. He didn't know many words of the Kiowan dialect, which was a form of the Athapaskan language. But he could usually make himself understood.

The brave nodded but said nothing. His dark eyes swept over the old buffalo hunter, the two nervous easterners, and the dead calves. Then he turned to Fargo.

"I am looking for big white hunter," he said in broken English, making a gesture with his hands to describe a large rectangle. "Scout. I am scout."

"You are looking for Duke Manning," Fargo said.

"Yes," the Kiowa smiled. "You know him? Big white hunter. Where is he?"

"Why do you look for him?" Fargo asked.

The brave's eyes narrowed, and his jaw jutted out.

"He will help my people," the Kiowa said at last. "Big white hunter is our friend. I must find him. Where is he?"

"What the hell is this all about?" cut in Mortimer Frank. "Who is this big hunter? Is this Indian alone?"

"Shut up," Fargo said.

"Alone. Yes," the Indian replied to the dandy. "I am scout."

Like hell you're alone, Fargo thought. The brave wasn't carrying food or water. He was a scout, traveling light. The rest of his party was probably just over the next rise.

"I know Duke Manning," said Fargo. "But I don't know where he is. And I don't think he is a friend of any Indian."

"You speak out of the wrong side of your mouth," the brave said. He turned and rode away.

Fargo heard the rifle being drawn at the same moment he heard Louis Vandermeer mutter, "I'm gonna get some Indian skin."

He turned in his saddle and saw the dandy raise the barrel and aim at the back of the retreating Kiowa brave. He fired.

The Kiowa scout slumped over, the wound in his back quickly darkening, spreading. The Indian's horse slowed and came to a halt.

"Well, I got me a redskin!" Louis Vandermeer whooped. He and the other easterner spurred their horses and sped over to investigate.

"I sure don't like that," the old buffalo hunter

said. "Killing Indians for sport ain't my line of work."

Fargo swore. He scanned the wide plains. The skinner's wagon was approaching just half a mile away now. Fargo's lake blue eyes continued to sweep the landscape. A moment later, he found what he was seeking and hoping not to find.

In the distance, a wavering dark line appeared as if out of nowhere. A line of mounted men—Kiowa warriors, he knew. More than a hundred. Coming straight for them.

5

The oncoming Kiowa warriors were still more than two miles distant but coming fast. The old buffalo hunter saw them.

"Oh hell," Fargo said. "Our best chance is to outrun them. They've come north from Kiowa territory, so they probably rode hard. If their horses are tired, we've got a chance."

"Yep," the old man agreed.

"Indians coming! Ride out!" Fargo shouted to the dandies, who were gingerly approaching the dead Kiowa. They started and turned around. Their smiles evaporated as they sighted the approaching braves. As they stared, frozen with fear, the scout lying across the neck of his mount raised himself, and summoning his last strength, lifted a wavering arm and threw a knife straight at Louis Vandermeer's back.

The blade struck and Vandermeer shrieked. His horse started forward as he fell, the Indian's knife half in him. He didn't know enough to kick his feet out, so one boot caught in his stirrup and he dragged along the ground beside his galloping horse, screaming and twisting. Blood and dirt quickly darkened his spotless new buckskin suit. He was done for, Fargo knew.

The other dandy, Mortimer Frank, clung to his horse, white-faced. He dug the long-roweled spurs into the bloodied ribs of his mount. The horse balked, then reared, came down to earth and reared again. The line of Kiowa warriors was galloping now, drawing closer.

The old buffalo hunter shouted and waved to his skinner's crew. The approaching men spotted the Indians, too, and quickly unhitched the horses from the wagon team and mounted them, speeding off in the opposite direction.

"Let's get out of here," the old buffalo hunter said to Fargo, glancing back at Mortimer Frank trying to control his rearing horse. The hunter galloped off after his men.

The Kiowa were close enough now that Fargo could see the individual warriors, their buffalo hide shields raised, rifles and bows at the ready. Mortimer Frank's horse continued to rear, wheeling on its hind legs, its eyes wild. Frank, panicked, dug his spurs again and again into the horse's sides in a vain effort to control it. He laid the quirt down across the horse's neck until it drew blood.

Fargo swore. He couldn't leave a defenseless man in the path of the oncoming Indians. He galloped over.

"Don't kick! You're making it worse! Pull her head down!" he shouted. If the man would just calm down and seize control of the frenzied horse . . .

But Mortimer Frank, wide-eyed and delirious, was beyond hearing or comprehending. He continued to dig into the horse's side with the cruel spurs as it bucked and danced, furiously whipping the horse with his quirt.

The Kiowa were close enough that Fargo heard their war cries.

"Follow me!" Fargo shouted in a last attempt to shake the man from his insane goading of his mount. He galloped off after the hunter and his crew.

The Ovaro leapt forward, and the yellow grasses became a blur. Fargo turned back and saw Mortimer Frank, still flailing at his horse. As he watched, the line of Kiowa approached and a score of arrows sailed through the air. Most of the arrows sank into Frank until he looked like a human pincushion. He rolled off his rearing horse, and the mount came to a standstill. The line of Kiowa swept around them, and Fargo turned back, concentrating on riding as fast as possible. He was catching up to the buffalo hunter and his crew, who were riding hell-bent.

After half a mile, Fargo glanced back again. They were pulling away from the pursuing Kiowa. The leader, a tall chief in a red feathered war bonnet, signaled the line to stop. They came to a ragged halt, some of the warriors continuing to ride beyond the line and then turning back, reluctantly.

Two white men had died in exchange for the Kiowa scout's life. They were avenged. And now they would turn away and seek other foes. The Cheyenne.

After a few more miles, the Kiowa were out of sight. Fargo pulled up. The buffalo hunter and his crew reined in as well.

"I think we're in the clear," Fargo said.

"The buffalo hunter removed his stained hat and wiped his face with a grimy bandanna.

"Guess so," he said. "Close call."

"Lost our clients though," one of the skinners said, looking back.

"We're all right," said the old hunter. "They paid half in advance. I guess we ought to get in town and buy us a new wagon. And find some more eastern dandies who want to get themselves some bison."

Fargo bid them goodbye and angled off to the west toward Reggio's Trading Post. The encounter with the hunters and the Kiowa had taken him farther north than he intended to go.

He glanced at the sun, just passing the zenith. He'd be at Reggio's by sunset if all went well. Fargo pulled some pemmican out of his saddlebag and chewed on it thoughtfully. He stopped at the next stream where he and the pinto drank the clear, cool water. Then he continued to ride through the warm autumn afternoon.

It was happening just as he feared it would. The Kiowa and Cheyenne on the warpath. And scared white men getting in the middle of it. And all of it senseless killing.

Now the Kiowa were north of the Arkansas River, looking for the Cheyenne no doubt. And looking for Duke Manning, Fargo thought, remembering the scout's words. Now what the hell did the Kiowa want with the man they called the big white hunter?

Fargo asked himself that question all the way to Reggio's Trading Post.

Reggio was slumped on a barrel, leaning against the building when Fargo galloped into the dusty yard. For a moment, Fargo feared the old hunchback was dead, but he suddenly jumped, raised his head and hurriedly limped across to Fargo. The golden red rays of the setting sun streaked the yard.

Fargo swung off the pinto just as the hunchback reached him.

"Thank heaven you're here!" Reggio said, his gnarled hands clutching at Fargo's arm.

"I got your message. You said your life was in danger."

"Oh yes," the man said, hanging his head. "My life is over. I am dead. Dead."

"What's this all about?" Fargo snapped. He led the pinto over to the water trough and tethered it while the hunchback walked along behind him.

"I . . . I have a confession to make . . ." Reggio began.

"Is it about Duke Manning?" Fargo asked.

"What do you know about that?"

"While I was standing outside your office door, I heard Duke say he was holding a note for ownership of the trading post."

"Oh that," the hunchback said, waving a tired hand. "That's nothing. Nothing." He bit his lip, and Fargo saw the old man was fighting to hold back tears, his old face twisting with emotion.

"What then?" he said.

"It's . . . it's my daughter."

"Gina?" Fargo said.

"How do you know her name?" Reggio asked, sudden suspicion in his eyes.

"I happened to be sitting on your roof the other day when you dropped in to visit her prison," Fargo snapped again. "Now, out with it. Where is she? Did Duke kidnap her?"

He felt rage rise within him as he imagined the slender blond young woman carried off by Duke Manning.

"Yes! I mean, no, no," Reggio said. "Not exactly." The old hunchback rubbed his head with one hand, pulled a folded piece of paper from his breast pocket, and handed it to Fargo. "She left this letter."

Fargo unfolded the paper and read it by the dying light of the sunset.

Father—You have kept me in this prison for too long. I know you think this is best for me, but it is not. I am sixteen and old enough to decide for myself now.

For a long time, I have been in love. But I could not tell you because you did not want to lose me and would never let me go anyway. So, tonight Duke Manning is taking me away forever. He is a wonderful man, tall, dark, handsome. He is strong and he leads other men.

I know you thought you were doing the best for me, but I could not live imprisoned anymore and I was beginning to hate you for it.

And I know that you were gambling. And you were losing the money that would have made it possible for us to escape this trading post. I did not want to be in this cage forever.

Please do not try to follow me. This is what I want and I am finally happy. Your daughter, Gina.

"I see," Fargo said, folding the paper and handing it back to Reggio. "She's run off with Duke Manning."

"Please get her back for me," the hunchback pleaded. "I'll pay you anything. Anything at all. You can have everything. The whole trading post. Just get my daughter back to me." Reggio's fingers plucked again at his sleeve.

Fargo glared at the old man. He didn't like the idea of Gina running off with scum like Duke Manning. On the other hand, she hadn't deserved to be kept a prisoner either. He knew he would go after her. Hell, he was going after Duke anyway for what he had done to Sylvia. But he found himself angry at the trader.

"So," Fargo said, "let me get this straight. If I get her back from Duke Manning, you'll coop her up again. And you'll have money left to get her out of here. You want her to grow up alone in some kind of prison? What kind of life is that?"

Reggio hung his head.

"What could I do?" he asked quietly. "If she had come into the trading post, some man would have . . . would have . . ."

"Rape?" Fargo said. "There were enough men around who would have come to her defense if you couldn't handle it alone. But I think you were really afraid she might have run off eventually and left you. That was it, wasn't it?"

The hunchback hung his head lower.

"Gina is all I have since her mother died," he said. "I was trying to protect her. From men who might be . . . unsuitable."

"She's almost a grown woman," Fargo said. "It's time she was learning to protect herself. But one thing has me puzzled. She said in the letter she had been in love for a long time. Did you let Duke Manning visit her back there?"

"Of course not!" Reggio said. "I ... I don't know how he found her. I guess the same way you did."

Fargo nodded thoughtfully.

"Where's Olive Parson?" he asked suddenly.

"She doesn't know anything about this," Reggio protested.

"I'd like to talk to her," Fargo said.

"She's out back."

Reggio led the way through the dark and deserted trading post and the few small rooms at the back that he and Olive used as living quarters. He paused at a large padlocked door, now open, and walked through the small sparsely furnished rooms which had been Gina's.

They walked out the rear door into the enclosed yard. Fargo looked around at the high board fence which surrounded it and the sky with the first stars coming out above. The bare yard looked even smaller and more desolate from the ground than it had from the vantage of the rooftop.

The thin figure of Olive Parson sat upright and alone under the tree.

"I hear Gina's gone," Fargo said.

The gray-haired woman looked at him.

"Hello, Mr. Fargo," she said stiffly. "Yes, she's run off with Mr. Manning. But I don't see what business that is of yours."

"Olive!" Reggio said. "Skye Fargo is going to help me get my daughter back. He's going to go after Duke Manning."

"Leave the girl alone," Olive said, her voice thin with anger. "She's finally got a chance to leave here. Let her go."

"Olive!" Reggio said. "Why Duke Manning . . . well, he kidnapped her!"

"Kidnapped! Pshaw!" Olive said. "You read her letter. He saved her from spinsterhood. A big, strong, handsome man like Duke Manning is a damn good catch for a girl like Gina. She could do a lot worse. I say you two men should stay out of her affairs. If Duke Manning finally asked her to marry him, then I think she should go off with him . . ." Olive's voice trailed off.

"Finally asked her to marry him?" Fargo repeated. "That's strange. Gina's letter didn't say anything about Duke finally asking her to marry him. What do you know about this?"

Olive's eyes shifted as she glanced from one man to the other.

"Well," she said briskly. "I guess he'll marry her. It's a natural assumption. She wouldn't just run off with a man unless he said he would. She would have gotten him to promise . . ."

"You got Manning to promise to marry her," Fargo cut in. "The whole thing happened because you thought Manning would be a good husband for Gina. You told her all about him. Then you started bringing him back here, with yourself as chaperon. I'll bet. You just couldn't wait to see the romance blossom, could you?"

"Love is a sacred thing," Olive said stiffly, her face red.

"And then Manning got too eager for you, didn't he?" Fargo taunted. "And when Manning said he'd marry her, I'll bet you helped her pack her bags."

"Olive!" Reggio said. "Can this be true?"

Olive Parson gestured around the fenced yard.

"What I did was for the best," Olive said. "The girl should get married while she has the chance. What kind of life is this for Gina?"

"And what kind of life will she have when Duke Manning gets tired of her and throws her out?" Fargo said hotly. He turned and marched out of the yard.

"Love conquers all!" he heard Olive call after him just as he entered the building.

Love indeed, he thought. Olive Parson was a dried out spinster who had used Gina to further her own romantic fantasies.

And Duke Manning was capable of one thing and one thing only: self-interest. That much was clear. Manning would lie, steal, and cheat to get what he wanted.

The question was, would Gina have enough sense to see through Duke Manning? Would she come to her senses, with a little persuasion, before it was too late?

Fargo mounted the pinto and galloped off across the darkening plains. He needed to find Duke Manning's tracks. And fast.

The sound of drunken singing carried a long way across the plains at night. Fargo heard the sound several miles ahead. He could tell by the moon it was close to midnight now.

As he had left the trading post at dusk, he had come across the deep ruts of Manning's wagons almost immediately. And the tracks led due north up into Cheyenne territory.

It hadn't been hard to follow them even in the darkness. The tracks led straight across the prairie, dipping down to cross the streams and cutting through the dust of the buffalo wallows, which had been dry since the early summer.

And now he had found their camp. He slowed.

Fargo leaned forward in the saddle, eyes and ears alert to everything around him. All was quiet except for the far-off voices of the men singing. Finally, he dismounted. He left the pinto standing, untethered, beside a low tangle of rabbit bush. The horse would graze and wouldn't stray. It would come when he whistled.

Fargo loosened the Colt in his holster and moved forward silently. The camp was in the bottom of a gully wash, beside a stream. As he drew nearer, he could see the low cutbank by the flickering light of the campfire.

He crouched low and moved ahead in short spurts, taking time to pause and survey the darkness around him. So far he had seen no lookouts. That meant either they were well hidden, or Manning was damned arrogant and didn't post any.

Fargo froze as a sudden movement ahead of him caught his attention and then relaxed as a coyote scampered away into the night. Just in front of him and not far from the camp was a grassy hillock. He headed for it, dropped to his knees, and slowly made his way through the tall grasses, careful not to make any of the tops move much more than they would in the night breeze. Finally, he came to the crest of the hillock and parted the grass so that he could look down into the camp.

The wagons stood end to end in a semicircle to one side, the horses hobbled nearby. The campfire was in the center, and a dirty canvas tent was pitched on the far end.

The smell of cooking was heavy in the air, and Manning's crew lay about the campfire, drinking, smoking, and singing. Duke sat on a large log, a whiskey bottle in one hand. He drained the remaining contents in one swig, tossing his head back, and then threw the empty bottle over his shoulder. His other huge arm was wrapped around Gina, who looked very pale and frightened as she huddled next to him.

Manning chucked her under the chin.

"What's the matter, my lady love?" he asked. "Don't you like your wedding party?"

The men laughed and began singing again, rolling about on the ground. They were very drunk, but Duke appeared to be in complete control of himself.

"It's just that ... we're not married yet!" Gina said. Fargo had to concentrate to make out her words above the din. "Olive said I had to have a proper wedding, with a minister, before we would be married. Olive said it has to be proper."

Duke smiled down at her.

"You are right, my dear," he said. "We should do the thing proper."

Several of the men sniggered.

"Hoagie!" Manning boomed. "You're a minister, aren't you?"

A man in a rumpled plaid shirt got to his feet and stood swaying in the firelight, a bottle clenched in his fist.

"Like hell I am," he said, thinking he was being insulted.

One of the other men got unsteadily to his feet and clung to Hoagie, whispering to him.

"Oh sure," Hoagie said after a moment. "I'm a preacher. Used to give those brimstone sermons in my little church down in Texas." Hoagie was getting carried away with himself. He took another pull from the bottle.

"Reverend Hoagie can still marry folks if he's got his collar on," said Manning, drawing Gina nearer him. "Ain't that right? Go fetch that collar that Simon borrows to wear in town."

The men were all on their feet now, laughing at this new game. One of them went to fetch Simon's detachable collar while someone else slicked Hoagie's hair down with a splash of the whiskey. They put the collar on backward on Hoagie, buttoning his plaid shirt to hold it on.

Manning pulled Gina to her feet.

"Come, my dear," he said grandly. "We'll be married here tonight out under the stars. Then we can enjoy . . ." The men sniggered again.

Gina drew away from Duke.

"It doesn't seem quite right," she said uncertainly. "There's supposed to be a ring. And we have to sign some papers."

"The ring!" Manning said. "Of course, my dearest. You must have a ring."

"I got one," one of the men said, stepping forward.

Manning took it and handed to Gina.

"Of course, I will buy you a diamond one when we come to the next town," he said. "Nothing is too expensive or too fine for my beautiful beloved."

The men exchanged looks of amusement as Gina looked up smiling at Manning.

"And we can sign the documents tomorrow," he said. "It's too dark tonight to trouble ourselves with that."

Manning led her forward to where Hoagie was standing beside the campfire. Hoagie was suddenly tongue-tied.

"We've come together," Manning started.

Hoagie nodded, unable to speak.

"To join this man and this woman . . ." Manning prodded.

Hoagie nodded again, his mouth gaping.

"In holy matrimony," Manning finished. He turned toward Gina. "Now I put the ring on you and say, "I do." Then you say it. I do." he said quickly.

"I do," she added under her breath. "But . . . but . . ."

"And now, Hoagie . . . the Reverend Hoagie will pronounce us man and wife," Manning said, prodding Hoagie.

"I pro . . . pronounce you man and wife," Hoagie said.

"And now, I may kiss the bride," Manning said. He bent down over the slender blond girl and kissed her deeply. Fargo saw her struggle against the gigantic man who held her in his powerful arms. The men whooped and cheered. Finally, Manning released her, and she stepped back, wiping her mouth against her sleeve, a look of terror and confusion on her face. She hadn't liked the kiss.

"Now, my wife, we can go into the tent for the night . . ."

Just then one of the men shouted, and Fargo heard the sounds of hoofbeats, coming fast. Three mounted braves rode up to the firelight. Kiowa. The men scrambled nervously for their rifles, and Gina stifled a scream, shrinking against the huge frame of Duke Manning.

"Friends!" Manning called out in the Kiowan dialect, gesturing for his men to put down their guns. "Why do you ride into my camp in the middle of the night?"

"Big white hunter," said one of the Kiowa, a muscled brave with blue feathers in his hair. "Chief Black Finger brings us north. We come to make war on our old friends, the Cheyenne."

"I have seen many Kiowa killed on the plains with Cheyenne arrows," said Manning.

Fargo started. So Manning had seen the dead Indians, after all. But at the trading post, he said he hadn't. Why had he lied?

"Yes," said the brave. "And the Cheyenne take all of the buffalo skins. So now, we will take scalps in return. First we must find the Cheyenne camp. You know where it is. Take us there."

Manning looked up at the mounted Indian.

"Yes," he said slowly. "I will do this for my old friends the Kiowa. We will go now in the dark, and I will show you where the Cheyenne sleep. In the morning, you can take many scalps easily."

The three Indians exchanged looks and nodded in agreement.

"Do you have to go with these Indians?" Gina asked, fear in her voice.

"Oh yes," said Manning grandly to the three Kiowa. "Let me introduce my new squaw."

The three braves looked down expressionless. Gina turned on her heels and fled into the tent while Duke Manning let out a roar of laughter.

One of the men brought Duke's saddled horse, and he mounted, following the braves out of the circle of firelight and across the plains. The rest of the men pulled their bedrolls out of the wagons and began making ready for sleep. Within a few minutes, most of them were snoring. Two men had walked up to the top of the bank to keep watch. They stood together, looking out at the plains and talking in low voices.

It was now or never, Fargo thought. He backed silently through the grass, and his long lean frame bent almost double, ran quickly around the periphery of the camp, coming to the rear of the tent.

He dropped to his knees, and keeping one eye on the backs of the watchman on the bank overhead, he slowly lifted one corner of the flap. Gina lay on blankets, tossing and turning in the darkness inside the canvas tent. By the sound of her steady breathing, Fargo knew she was asleep, exhausted from the day's travel and uncertainty. But it was a restless sleep and she would awaken at the slightest sound.

Fargo stole forward silently, easing himself inside the tent beside the sleeping girl. He very quietly laid a hand over her mouth, and she jerked awake, her eyes wide with fright.

"Don't make a sound," he whispered. "My name is Skye Fargo. Your father sent me to take you back home."

Her eyes blinked a few times, and her body relaxed slightly as she took in the words.

"Promise you won't scream?" he asked. When she nodded, he took his hand slowly away. She swallowed.

"How did you get in here?" She sat up.

"Never mind," he said. "There's no time for you to get dressed. We have to get out of here."

Gina started to make a move and then stopped.

"To go back to my father and be imprisoned?" she asked, her voice low. "Even if I wanted to, I can't. I am now married to Duke Manning."

"I saw that sham wedding that Duke put you through," Fargo said. "You're no more married than I am."

Gina looked up at him searchingly.

"But, Duke said he loved me," she said. "That I'm the only woman he has ever loved and ever will love. And . . . love conquers all, doesn't it?" Fargo heard the tears that threatened to choke her voice.

"That's a hill of beans," Fargo said roughly. "And Olive Parson has been filling your head with a bunch of romantic hooey. Look, Gina," he said, adopting a more kindly tone, "you've got to face facts. Duke Manning is a no good son of a bitch. He's pulled a fast one on you. If you have any sense, you'll get out now."

Gina seemed to waver for a moment.

"I . . . I don't know," she said. "Why should I believe you anyway? I don't even know you. And anyway, Olive knows Duke, and she said he would be a good husband for me. And that I shouldn't wait until it was too late. No, I'll stay here. And I'll talk to Duke when he comes back."

"Gina," Fargo said, rising to his feet in the

cramped tent, "you've got to be reasonable. Come with me."

He put out his hand to help her up.

"If you so much as touch me, I'll scream bloody murder," she said. Fargo seized her arm.

6

Gina's mouth opened to scream, but Fargo was quicker. His hand closed around the butt of his Colt, which he brought out of its holster in a flash, twirled half around, and clubbed her as lightly as he could on the back of the skull. She slumped forward.

Fargo reached down and grasped her slender waist, hoping he had managed to hit her hard enough to keep her out for a while, but not too hard to do any damage. She'd have a helluva headache in the morning. But he figured it'd be better than waking up in bed with Duke Manning.

She was light as a feather. He slung her over one shoulder, marveling at her slender legs beneath her white cotton gown. He eased himself out of the rear of the tent, glancing up to see only one of the watchmen still on the bank above. The man's back was still toward the campfire.

With a hasty glance about him, Fargo started forward, making toward the cover of the hillock. He raced up the short rise and suddenly ran straight into the other watchman, wandering back toward camp.

"What the hell?" the man shouted, seeing Fargo with the girl draped over his shoulder.

Fargo didn't pause, but barreled toward him, giving the man a sudden uppercut with his fist as he came within striking distance. The watchman went down heavily, and Fargo ran by him into the darkness. Behind him, he heard voices of some of the men, roused by the watchman's shout. Then a shot was fired, and he heard the voices of pursuit.

As he ran, Fargo licked his lips, puckered, and blew. No sound came out. Damn hard to whistle at a full run, he thought.

He paused a moment and tried again. This time, the whistle sounded from his lips, low and distinct. It would carry for a long distance. Fargo ran on and in a moment, he heard the hoofbeats of the trusty Ovaro approaching.

Fargo threw Gina over the saddle and leapt on just as the bullets began whizzing around him. The men on foot were just behind and he could hear others who had mounted racing toward him.

He galloped straight away from the camp into the moonlit night. The bullets zinged by. He hunched down, holding the unconscious girl across the saddle in front of him.

The pinto took long strides, its powerful legs churning the dark grass. They pulled gradually away from Manning's men. The sturdy Ovaro could outrun almost any horse in the West.

When they drew out of firing range, Fargo sat upright and pulled Gina closer as they galloped along. He managed to get one of her legs over the saddle by hiking her gown up her thighs. Her legs were shapely and pale. She groaned once and slumped against his chest. He held her against him, his arms around her as they rode.

It was a helluva situation, he thought as he rode

the Ovaro across the dark prairie. The sounds of the men pursuing him grew more distant. He turned in the saddle and could just barely make them out, a dark moving shape on the plains behind him, all in a clump. They were too stupid to spread out, he saw. He smiled to himself.

He galloped to the top of a long slope, and just over the summit, suddenly angled sharp to the right. By the time Manning's men reached that crest, he would be out of sight in a direction they wouldn't expect. He was galloping due north now, toward the dippers which hung low in the sky before him.

A dark gully appeared before him, and Fargo reined in the pinto. It slid down the bank and came to a halt. He paused, his ears alert to the sounds around him.

Behind him, he heard the hoofbeats and shouts of Manning's men. They knew they had lost him, but they continued in the same direction. They would ride all night, if necessary, trying to find him. Fargo imagined Duke Manning's wrath when he returned to find Gina had been snatched away. The sounds died out finally, and the night was still.

Fargo emerged from the gully and looked behind him. On the moonlit plain, all was quiet. He continued north.

Manning and the Kiowa braves had gone this way. The autumn camp of Broken Bow's band lay in this direction, he remembered. They pitched their tepees on a grassy wash, half hidden by a bluff beside what the Cheyennes called Old Blood Creek. It was an ideal location because the camp was practically invisible until you rode into the middle of it. Nevertheless, the cautious Chief Broken Bow always posted lookouts a mile from the camp in all directions. Fargo remembered Yellow Dog boasting that the Cheyenne had never suffered a surprise attack in camp.

But a hundred Kiowa warriors who knew exactly where the camp lay and attacked at dawn would slaughter Broken Bow's tribe.

The Indian camp was an hour's ride, Fargo figured. There was just enough time to warn the Cheyenne before the Kiowa attacked at first light.

If he didn't run into the Kiowa first, he thought, and his mouth tightened grimly. The Kiowa would probably attack from the south, sneaking up the creekbed. He swung the Ovaro out into a wide western arc that would carry them to the north side of the camp. When it seemed they had traveled far enough, Fargo turned the pinto back to the east, hoping the Cheyenne camp was where he remembered it.

They came to the creek bed a half hour later, and Fargo felt the hope rise in him. They were surely north of Broken Bow's camp. He followed the creek downstream, keeping watch for the Cheyenne lookouts.

Just as the banks grew steeper and the bed widened, a figure suddenly rose out of the grasses before him.

"Friend," Fargo said hastily in Algonquian, hoping the brave was Cheyenne. "I am Fargo, friend of Broken Bow. I come with a big message for him."

The brave was wary and kept his bow drawn. He yipped suddenly, like a coyote, and a moment later two other braves appeared from opposite directions, plunging down the banks. Fargo repeated his words. One of the braves sprinted into the darkness in the direction of the camp. The second gestured for Fargo to follow. The third disappeared into the darkness, and Fargo knew he had gone to see if Fargo had come alone.

The Ovaro walked surefootedly along the bank of the stream until Fargo saw in the moonlight ahead of him the grove of cottonwood trees that hid the camp. He rode into the deeper darkness beneath the branches until he realized he was suddenly surrounded by the dark shapes of the tepees.

A golden triangle appeared in the darkness, which blinked as dark shapes moved across it. Fargo's eyes made out the opening of a tepee, the interior lit by a fire. Indians were assembling inside. Several dark figures came near and stood silently.

He dismounted, pulling Gina off the Ovaro and holding her in his arms. She moaned once and then came to, suddenly struggling in his arms.

"You're safe now," he said, holding her close as she gradually calmed down.

"Where . . . where am I?" she said. Her hand moved to her head, and she tried to look around her.

"We're in an Indian camp," he said slowly. She stiffened. "But don't worry. They are friendly. We'll be safe here for the moment."

Suddenly he felt her shake, and then she began to cry, turning her face toward his chest and clutching him with both hands. He knew what she was crying about—the fear and the turmoil of the day, of running away from her father and of finding herself with Duke Manning, a man she hardly knew but idealized. The sobs racked her as she clung helplessly to him. Fargo waited a moment and then let her down gently so that she stood on her feet. She sniffled.

"You'll be all right," he said. One of the dark figures stepped forward from the shadows, and Fargo could see it was a woman.

"I will care for her," the woman said, leading Gina away. Another figure stepped forward and led Fargo toward the lighted entrance of the tepee.

Fargo stooped to enter and then found himself in the lighted warmth. A circle of braves sat cross-legged on buffalo robes. Yellow Dog was there. Fargo nodded to him. An old man, his face as carved with lines as a dry streambed, sat with his eyes closed. It was Broken Bow. One of the braves drew the flap closed behind him, and Fargo sat down.

"Greetings to Chief Broken Bow," Fargo said. He opened his mouth to speak of the impending attack, but the old chief opened his eyes and cut in.

"Old friend, Skye Fargo," he said. His voice was barely a whisper. "You have not come to our fire for many years. Since you brought Ten Claws back to our camp. Why do you ride under the moon?"

"The Kiowa have brought a hundred men from the south," Fargo said. "I have seen them. And at dawn, they will attack. They are being led by one called Black Finger."

The braves murmured among themselves, and

Broken Bow closed his eyes slowly, like a turtle resting in the sun. There was a long silence.

"But how can Black Finger know where we camp?" Broken Bow said, his eyes still closed. "I have known Black Finger for many years. But he has never come to our camp. Only a few friends know this place. But not the Kiowa. We have a treaty with them, but they do not know our tepee place."

"Duke Manning is bringing them here," Fargo said. "Tonight I was spying on his camp. Three Kiowa braves rode in. They called him the Big White Hunter and Friend of the Kiowa. They asked him to show them where the Cheyenne sleep. And then they rode off together."

"I don't believe you!" Yellow Dog said. "You lie. Duke Manning is the friend of the Cheyenne. He gives us buffalo meat."

"He lets you pick up the buffalo meat he's going to let rot," Fargo said. "He buys your friendship for nothing. He can leave the buffalo meat to the vultures. Or to the Cheyenne."

Yellow Dog's black eyes flashed. He half rose and Broken Bow raised his hand, eyes still closed. Yellow Dog sank back down, but his face was dark with fury.

"So," Broken Bow said. "One white man is lying. One is telling the truth. But which one?"

His eyes slowly opened again. They were milky white, almost sightless, Fargo guessed. Yet, as the chief turned his face toward Fargo, he seemed to stare right through him.

"Who is the squaw?" Broken Bow asked.

"Manning stole her. She is Reggio's daughter," Fargo explained. "I am taking her back to him.

But that's not important right now. What's important is that one hundred Kiowa warriors are about to attack. Your people will be slaughtered unless you do something."

The chief nodded.

"His words are true," Broken Bow said. "I believe the Kiowa are coming."

"An hour ago, one of the watchers thought he saw someone," one of the braves said. "But when he went to look, he saw nothing."

"Kiowa move with the shadows," Broken Bow said. "They will wait beyond our lookouts until light comes," the old chief said and nodded thoughtfully to himself. "Kiowa have been killing our people. And I do not understand why. They take buffalo robes. They do not take scalps. They leave their weapons and their arrows like spoor for us to read. Maybe the Kiowa have gone crazy."

Broken Bow paused, and his eyes closed again.

"Maybe the world has gone crazy," the old chief murmured. "Many times in my dreams I see the buffalo dying. I see the hunting grounds of my people with no deer. No buffalo. But I do not understand how. There are so many buffalo that they are like the stars in the sky. But in my dreams, they are all gone."

Some of the younger braves around the fire exchanged looks of impatience at the old man's words. Yellow Dog had had enough.

"I say we should attack the Kiowa!" said Yellow Dog. "They have broken the treaty. They have taken our robes. They should die. The Cheyenne are warriors. We must not run away like women. We must fight! Enough of peace. The Kiowa are now our enemies! I say we fight!"

Several of the braves around the fire muttered and nodded, agreeing with Yellow Dog.

"What do you say, Skye Fargo?" Broken Bow asked suddenly. Fargo saw his eyes open a slit, the firelight glittering in them.

"I have seen Kiowa braves dead, too," Fargo said. "With Cheyenne weapons in them. Who is breaking the treaty?"

Broken Bow's eyes opened again.

"I have not seen this. Who is killing Kiowa?" he asked, his voice suddenly resonant and full as Fargo had remembered it from years before. The braves looked at one another. "Yellow Dog, answer me," Broken Bow said. "Do you kill Kiowa?"

"No," Yellow Dog spat. "I want to kill Kiowa. But I do not. But my heart dances to see the dead Kiowa with Cheyenne arrows in them."

Fargo knew Yellow Dog was not lying. If he had killed Kiowa, he would admit it to the chief, his father. Then who was killing the Indians?

Fargo thought of Duke Manning and his men. They could easily be ambushing lone Indians on the plains. They could be taking the robes. But Fargo doubted the Cheyenne would believe this. And what would Duke Manning gain by starting a full-scale Indian war? It didn't make sense.

Fargo shook his head.

"Yellow Dog," he said, "when I saw you on the trail to Reggio's, I showed you how to mark your robes. Are all the Cheyenne robes marked?"

Yellow Dog nodded. He pulled back the robe he was sitting on, and Fargo saw the three small, almost invisible dots on the center of the tanned hide.

"Every Cheyenne robe is marked," Yellow Dog

said. "But we will find them with the Kiowa. They are stealing our skins."

Fargo nodded. Time was fleeting. It was just an hour before dawn. One of the braves reached for a parfleche and withdrew the long pipe and began to stuff it with tobacco. Fargo knew that the pipe would make its round now. They were wasting time here. The Cheyenne needed to be making their escape.

"The Kiowa are coming," Fargo said impatiently. "If we sit here and do nothing, everyone will be slaughtered."

Chief Broken Bow nodded slowly and made a gesture with his hand. One of the braves left the tepee.

"We will smoke now," Broken Bow said firmly. "You are honored guest. Ten summers have passed since you brought Ten Claws back to the tribe. Today you bring us news about the Kiowa. Today is a day to call the spirits."

And Fargo knew that there was nothing more he could say. It would be against the rigid laws of Indian etiquette to leave the tent just as the pipe began to make its slow circle. But as soon as possible, he would leave the tepee, retrieve Gina, and get the hell out before the shooting started. He swore to himself as he watched each of the braves take a slow smoke and pass on the pipe. Finally, it reached him, and he took an impatient draw.

"Our old friend is in a hurry," Broken Bow said. "It is better to go slowly and enjoy."

Fargo exhaled and took another draw on the pipe. Slowly this time. Then he passed it on to the next brave who smiled at him.

Finally the pipe returned to Broken Bow who packed it into the parfleche.

"Let us go now," Broken Bow said, rising laboriously to his feet. Fargo was among the first to exit the tepee. He was surprised to find his pinto standing by the entrance, along with other Indian ponies. The first hint of light was in the eastern sky. Fargo blinked and looked around. The tepees were gone. All except Broken Bow's. While they had been smoking the pipe, the tribe had packed up the camp and stolen silently away. Fargo figured they had probably headed north. Broken Bow came up behind him, leaning on the arm of Yellow Dog.

"Now I will leave a sign for my old friend Black Finger," he said. One of the braves handed him two arrows which he broke over his knee and laid on the ground. "Two broken arrows. He will know that I wish to speak to him here in two days."

The old chief turned away, just as braves removed the robes from his tepee and quickly folded the lodge poles. The fire had already been extinguished.

"The girl will be waiting for you one hour up the creek," Broken Bow said. "Thank you for telling us the Kiowa come."

Fargo nodded.

"I hope you and Black Finger can find peace," Fargo said. He heard the faint twitter of a bird in the cottonwood tree above.

"We must go," the chief said. Fargo moved away and mounted the Ovaro.

For the better part of an hour, he galloped up the streambed alongside the Cheyenne as the dawn brightened. Then they angled off across the prairie. A few moments later, he saw two ponies standing beneath a stand of serviceberry bushes. He reined in.

Gina sat astride one horse, looking drawn and weak. A brave sat astride the second horse, and the Indian woman who had taken her away earlier stood with the reins of Gina's mount in her hand. Fargo dismounted and led the Ovaro forward.

"Your tribe has gone to the east, across the plains," Fargo said in Algonquian.

"We know," said the woman. She stepped forward from the shadows, and Fargo saw her more clearly. Her face was round and smooth, the brows lifting in dark arches above two flashing black eyes. Her white deerskin dress, beaded and belted, clung to her high breasts and her slender waist. The slit up one side showed her slender and muscular legs. "You do not know me?" she said.

"Ten Claws!" he said, stepping forward. She moved toward him as he embraced her, feeling for an instant the softness of her womanliness as he held her in his arms. She stepped back.

He looked at her again, trying to meld the picture of the fierce six-year-old girl he had saved ten years ago with the lovely, graceful creature she had become.

"The white woman is very tired," Ten Claws said, pointing to Gina. "She cannot travel much further." Fargo glanced up and saw that she was right. Gina, exhausted physically and emotionally, could barely sit upright in the saddle. The bump on the head he had given her probably didn't help, he thought ruefully. He noted that they had given her a buckskin dress to wear to replace her flimsy cotton nightdress.

"Nearby is a place we will be safe for a while," Ten Claws said. "We will take you there."

Fargo nodded, looking out across the vastness as the first rays of the rising sun reached across the rippling grass. An hour's ride behind them, the Kiowa would be riding into the deserted Cheyenne camp. They would find the two broken arrows left behind and know that Broken Bow wished to talk. But they might send tracking parties out anyway to catch any stragglers from the camp.

"We had better hide our tracks," Fargo said.

Ten Claws nodded. She led Gina's horse toward the stream, Fargo followed, and the brave fell in behind them. Ten Claws was wise in the ways of tracking and hiding tracks, Fargo saw. She hiked up her skirt, revealing her slender thighs and plunged into the water, wetting her mocassins. Then she surefootedly led them up the stream where they would leave no tracks. They turned off into a deep branch of the stream, which narrowed, the clay banks rising high around them. Then they made another branching until they stood in a gully, like a miniature canyon, filled with rabbit bush and rangy scrub oak which would easily hide their horses.

The brave dismounted instantly and quickly climbed up the bank. He sat on the lip of the gully, partially hidden by the low grasses. If anyone tracked them, or wandered near, he would see them.

"There are caves here in the bank, where we can rest until dark," Ten Claws said, pointing.

Fargo dismounted and let the Ovaro wander toward a green patch of sweetgrass. Then he turned and lifted Gina off the horse. Her eyes were still dazed and she clung to him for a moment, reluctant to let go. Ten Claws took blankets from the other horse and led Gina into the bushes. In a few moments, she returned.

"The white woman needs rest. Then she will recover."

Fargo nodded.

"We can't risk a fire," Fargo said. He pulled pemmican, jerky, and some hardtack out of his saddlebag and offered it to Ten Claws. She smiled and took several pieces. They sat on a rock and talked as the sun rose and the morning light gradually filled the small gully. Fargo told her about the trading post and The Gilded Cage. About Gina running away with Manning. Ten Claws told him about the hunting and how the buffalo did not always come as they used to. As the morning grew warmer, the mockingbirds and meadowlarks twittered and they fell silent.

Fargo's thoughts were full of the events of the last day, of Duke Manning, the way he strong-armed Sylvia and Reggio, and the attack of the Kiowa on the Cheyenne camp. He'd saved Gina from Manning and had averted the slaughter of Broken Bow's tribe. At least for the moment.

But Manning was still on the loose. And he had been too slick to get caught. Manning hadn't kidnapped Gina. She had run away with him. And, so far, Fargo hadn't been able to convince her that Duke was up to no good.

And then there was Reggio. He had been stupid to give Manning a note of ownership of his trading post. Manning was threatening him with it. And yet, Reggio didn't believe Fargo when he told him Manning and his men were cheating at dice. Manning was slick. That was for certain.

And he'd been slick with Sylvia, too. She couldn't prove extortion against Manning. She had signed over twenty percent of her business and now there wasn't a goddamn thing she could do about it.

And then there were the Indians. Yellow Dog still didn't quite believe that Manning had brought the Kiowa to their camp. Maybe Broken Bow saw it, but Yellow Dog seemed convinced that Manning was the tribe's loyal friend. There was no way to prove anything against Manning.

Fargo sighed and leaned back against the sun-warmed rock. Ten Claws rested her hand lightly on his knee, and he glanced over at her. She smiled shyly.

Fargo leaned over and pulled her closer to him. Her dark eyes said yes, and he kissed her, small nibbling kisses at first and then deeper ones, exploring her mouth with his tongue.

She reached up and pulled the bands from her hair, undoing her braids and letting her long dark hair fall loose around her. She was beautiful, her face as smooth as unrippled water, her dark eyes deep.

"Skye Fargo is tired. He thinks too much," she said. "Come with me, and I will make him rested." She stood and pulled on his hand to follow her. Fargo got to his feet, and she led the way through the dense underbrush to a wall of the clay bank. In the shade, a smooth, shallow cave cut into the earth. Fargo saw that Ten Claws had already arranged blankets there. He smiled. Yes, rest would do him good.

He pulled her down beside him and removed his boots, stretching out in the damp coolness of the cave. Ten Claws lay down beside him, and he kissed her again, deeply, banishing the troubling thoughts, banishing everything but the taste and feel and smell of her. She moaned and sought his hand, pulling it up her firm thigh. He felt himself stiffen, his maleness ready for her.

His hand slowly explored upward, felt softness, wetness, the brush of her fur. Then he slipped his fingers inside her, gently, exploring her mouth with his, while she writhed beneath him. She struggled to pull her dress upward and then broke away from him to pull it over her head so that she suddenly lay beside him, bronzed, soft, and smooth and completely naked.

He took in the sight of her large firm breasts with their dark brown nipples. He kissed down her neck and shoulders and breasts and slender waist until he caught a whiff of musk and then nuzzled into her mound as she stifled a cry. She muttered in Algonquian as he licked and sucked on her and struggled to get out of his jeans and shirt. Finally, he lifted himself above her, and she looked downward, her eyes widening at the sight of his hugeness, and she reached down to grasp it, guiding it as he sank down on top of her, burying his face in the herbal sweetness of her black hair as he felt her slender legs open and wrap themselves around him.

She was warm and wet, strong and tight. He pushed against her, feeling her buck beneath him, meeting him thrust for thrust, grunting softly each time. He reached beneath her to grasp her firm buttocks as he pushed, deeper inside her. He felt her hands on his back and a burning where her nails dug into him, helpless with passion.

"Oh, oh, ah," she cried in the universal language of pleasure.

She tossed her head from side to side as he continued to plunge inside, deeper and more forcefully. Nothing existed but this woman beneath him, this moment in which he would give it to her, deep between her legs, and would erupt like a hot volcano into her. She suddenly gasped, her eyes wide, and bit her lip.

"Yes, yes," she said in Algonquian, and he pushed his shaft into her again and felt the explosive spurting deep inside as she shuddered beneath him.

She was panting as he slowed, her hands dropped from around his back. He relaxed and rolled off of her to lay beside her on the blanket. The shade-cooled air wafted over him.

"I have thought so many times of the big man who saved my life when I was a girl," Ten Claws said. "Many times I have dreamed of this."

Fargo smiled at her. Ten Claws blinked sleepily as he adjusted his arm to cradle her head. Yes, sleep, he thought as his eyes closed. To gather strength for what would come. And, at the moment, that seemed very far away.

He awoke in midafternoon, stretching his long muscular body as he lay on the cool earth ledge. Ten Claws came awake beside him and sat up.

"We must now join our tribe," she said, looking

out at the branch-choked gully, touched with the yellows of early autumn.

She rose and quickly donned her buckskin dress. Fargo pulled on his drawers and jeans, then reached for his shirt. Ten Claws laughed when she saw his back.

"I have left my mark on you," she said.

Fargo rubbed his back with one hand and then looked at the palm to find small streaks of blood. He laughed, too.

"Ten Claws," he said. "You are well named."

They were still laughing when they came out of the bushes, Fargo still buttoning his shirt, to find Gina sitting on a rock beside the stream. The brave sat still on the top of the bank. Gina looked up as they approached, and her face darkened.

"How do you feel?" Fargo asked.

"My head hurts," she muttered. Gina flashed an angry look at Ten Claws, whose face remained impassive. She glanced from Fargo to Ten Claws and back again. From the look on her face, it was clear she knew what they had been up to. "I demand that you take me back to my husband," she said.

Fargo shook his head.

"Gina, Duke Manning is not your legal husband," he said. "That was no preacher and that was no wedding last night. And Duke Manning is no fit man for a girl like you."

Gina bit her lip and tears started to her eyes.

"He said he loved me," she said in almost a wail. "And I said 'I do.' So, even if I don't want to go back to Duke, I have to, don't I?"

Fargo heard the confusion in her words. She doubted Manning, but she wasn't sure. Ten Claws watched them both, unable to follow the English words, but understanding the conversation nevertheless.

"You don't have to do anything you don't want to do," Fargo said. "I'll take you back to your father, if you want."

"No!" Gina said vehemently. "He'd only imprison me again."

Fargo thought for a moment. Maybe it was better if she didn't go right back to Reggio's. Let the old hunchback sweat it awhile. Maybe he'd learn his lesson that his daughter needed some freedom in order to grow up.

But, Fargo thought, he couldn't very well haul Gina around with him. And he couldn't leave her with the Cheyenne, even though they would take good care of her. Gina needed some time to sort things out.

He thought of Sylvia. He'd take her to The Gilded Cage. It certainly wasn't an ideal spot for a virginal young lady, but he doubted the experience of seeing the sporting life for a day or two would do her much harm. And a sensible woman like Sylvia might be able to knock some common sense into Gina, which he had failed to do.

"I'll take you to town. You can stay with a woman friend of mine," he suggested, "until you decide what you want to do next."

"Oh, that would be perfect!" Gina said. Her face brightened and she dried her tears.

Perfect, Fargo thought. That might not be the word she would use when they got to The Gilded Cage, but he'd cross that bridge when they came to it.

In half an hour, they had eaten, watered the horses, saddled, and packed.

Gina hoisted herself onto the Ovaro, where she would ride with Fargo. He stood beside Ten Claws and looked down at her for a silent moment.

"We will meet again," she said. "Our fire always welcomes you." Fargo bent down and kissed her gently.

Ten Claws turned and gracefully mounted. She and the brave rode out of the gully, to follow their tribe.

Fargo mounted behind Gina, and the Ovaro picked its way down the streambed. Then they climbed a gentle bank and began to gallop across the open plain toward McKinney.

Fargo kept a sharp eye out, approaching the crests of hills slowly, pausing occasionally to listen to the wind. But there were no signs of the Kiowa warriors.

For the first hour, Gina sat stiffly in front of him, not saying a word. He could guess what she was thinking.

"Why did you kiss that Indian?" she said at last.

"Ten Claws is an old friend of mine," he answered.

"Are you going to marry her?" Gina asked after a time, sounding a bit worried.

Fargo laughed.

"I'm not the marrying kind," he said.

"Oh," she said. After a few more miles, she relaxed, resting back against his broad chest as the miles sped beneath them.

She was willow slender, he thought, as he felt her narrow back against him. But still a little girl in so many ways. She had a lot of growing up to do.

The sun was setting, and McKinney was an hour ahead. Fargo's lake blue eyes swept the peachblow clouds. In the distance, dots of blackness swirled like ashes above a campfire. Wheeling hawks. He knew it was another kill. Fargo loosened the Colt in his holster and tightened his arms around the slender girl in the saddle in front of him. He'd have to go look. He had to know.

A mile further on, Fargo dismounted.

"Stay here," Fargo said to Gina. She nodded, her mouth tight and her eyes fearful. He walked to the body and the vultures flapped into the air as he approached. The Cheyenne brave lay facedown in the grass. An empty travois lay on the ground nearby. A knife was plunged into his back up to the hilt. A yellow-and-blue leather ornament dangled from the hilt. Kiowa, of course.

But Fargo saw that the knife had not killed the Indian. The brave had been shot in the back of the neck. Point-blank range. Whoever killed him, had been standing real close. Close enough to talk. Until the Indian had turned his back. And after shooting him, the murderer plunged a Kiowa knife in the dead brave's back.

No Kiowa would waste a knife like that. And, with Kiowa on the warpath, no lone Cheyenne brave would stop to parley with Kiowa on the open plains.

As Fargo walked slowly back to Gina waiting on the pinto, he thought of Duke Manning again. He was certain the buffalo hunter was responsible for the killings. The Indians trusted Manning. They would stop to talk to him. And they trusted him so much, they would even turn their backs on him.

But why would Manning go to all the trouble to murder Cheyenne and Kiowa and provoke tribal warfare? Surely not just to steal a few buffalo skins? It didn't make sense.

Fargo mounted the Ovaro and headed toward McKinney. Gina didn't ask any questions, and Fargo's thoughts darkened as the dusk gathered.

It was nighttime and The Gilded Cage was crowded when they rode up in front. Fargo dismounted, tethered the Ovaro, and lifted Gina down. She was as limp as a rag doll, unused to long hours in the saddle and utterly exhausted.

"The owner of this . . . bar . . . is named Sylvia," Fargo said. He'd explain The Gilded Cage more fully to her in the morning. "She'll give you a warm bath, some fresh clothes and a nice quiet room for the night."

Gina nodded, bleary-eyed, and he held her close to him as they made their way toward the steps of the wide porch. Just then, two women, giggling, pushed through the batwing doors, a tall brunette in green and a small shapely figure in a bright yellow dress.

"Sylvia!" Fargo called.

She spotted him and her face lit up. She hurried across the porch.

"Skye!" she said. "Am I glad to see you here! Guess . . ." Her voice trailed away as she noticed Gina. "You poor dear," she murmured.

"She needs some food and rest," Fargo said. .

"Of course!" Sylvia answered. "Arabella, would you take this poor child upstairs and give her the spare room in the back. Tell Cook to send up some dinner and a bath."

The tall brunette took Gina's arm and was leading her away when Sylvia turned back to Skye.

"I'm so glad you're here," she said, laying a hand on his arm. "Guess who's upstairs? That bastard, Duke Manning!"

At the sound of his name, Gina whirled around, her eyes flashing.

"Duke? Duke is here? Please, take me to him!"

7

"Please, please," Gina repeated, approaching Sylvia and clutching at her arm, "I must see Duke. I must talk to him."

Sylvia raised her eyebrows and patted the shoulder of the half-hysterical girl.

"Now, honey," she said. "Why in blue blazes would you want to talk to that low-life scum?"

Gina's mouth gaped for a moment as she took in Sylvia's words.

"Why, he's my husband. Or . . . well, we're married," Gina said. "He told me I was the only woman for him and that he loved me . . ." She stopped, uncertainty in her voice.

Sylvia nodded slowly.

"I see," she said. "Well, honey, he's busy right now. Maybe you'd better wait until he comes downstairs."

"Maybe it would be better if she went upstairs," Fargo said. Sylvia looked at him surprised. "I don't think Gina knows Duke as well as she thinks she does," he added.

Sylvia pressed her lips tight.

"Who is Duke on top of tonight?" she asked, turning to the brunette.

"Hmm . . . I think he's got Priscilla. Yes, I'm

sure of it because I heard Prissy complaining she was going to take a lot of abuse and then he'd be slipping away without paying. And you'd have to be making up the difference like you always do."

Gina gasped, unwilling to take in what the two women were talking of.

"Duke's a regular here," Sylvia said to her. "We know him real well. You still want to go upstairs?"

Gina nodded her head affirmatively.

They were an odd foursome, Fargo thought, as he followed the three woman through the crowded bar and up the stairs. Several men looked up and saw Fargo going upstairs with Sylvia, Arabella, and one very young girl in buckskins.

"Hope you have a helluva time!" one of the men shouted, raising his half-empty glass.

"I plan to!" Fargo shouted back. He saw Gina blush deeply.

Sylvia led them down the papered hallway and opened a door that led to a narrow dead-end corridor, lit by a dim oil lamp. Cloaks hung on a row of hooks, and several boxes of supplies were piled at one end. Sylvia closed the door behind them, turned, and removed a framed picture from a wall to reveal a small sliding door, the size of a picture postcard, built into the wall.

Fargo chuckled.

"Why, Sylvia, can you spy on all the rooms like this?" he whispered. He could hear muffled voices from the next room.

"Damn right," she said. "Just don't be telling anybody about it. Now, once I open this little door, we have to be quiet."

Sylvia blew out the oil lamp and slid open the

door. Immediately, they heard Manning's booming voice.

Gina stood on tiptoe and peered through. Fargo could not see into the room, but the light lit Gina's face and he watched as two tears trickled down her cheeks.

"Why, Prissy, I think of you all the time when I'm out there hunting that buffalo. I think of your pretty tits. I think of your beautiful ass . . . ," Manning was saying.

"Oh, you say that to everybody."

"Well, that may be so," Manning answered, "but I mean it with you. Come on, let's go one more time."

"Duke, you remember what Sylvia said tonight. One time. And you gotta start paying us again."

"Like hell I do!" Manning roared. "Come on, Prissy . . ."

Gina turned away from the square of light, and Sylvia quietly shut it. They made their way back out into the hallway.

"Take Gina to the rear room upstairs," Sylvia said. Arabella nodded and led her off.

"Tonight I put my foot down," Sylvia said as she led Fargo down the corridor. "I told Duke that if he didn't start paying us again, he could never come back."

"And his answer?"

"Oh, Skye," she sighed, "he said he'd use the paper I signed to close us down for good. In one day's time. I sent one of the girls over to find Sheriff Smythe, but he's gone down to Texas about some stagecoach holdup. Straver and the troops are out in Colorado. And Major Brimwell . . ."

"Is good for nothing," Fargo finished her sentence.

"Can he really close me down?"

"If that document gives him part ownership of The Gilded Cage," Fargo said, "he probably can shut you down. It's legal and he'll get away with it."

Sylvia put her face in her hands.

"I'll lose everything. Once I pay the girls, I won't have enough to start a ranch like I always planned."

Fargo put an arm around her shoulder.

"Leave Duke Manning to me," he said, his voice cold. Inside, he felt himself boil with suppressed rage against the swaggering man inside that room. There seemed to be no way to catch Duke. There was no way to stop him. He would just have to take him head-on, man to man. Fargo ground his teeth as he had the pleasurable thought of his fist smashing through the bone of Duke Manning's face. "I'll be waiting downstairs for him."

When Manning walked down the staircase, he was laughing and buttoning his vest. His deep brown eyes swept the crowded room and locked onto Skye Fargo's piercingly cold gaze as he stood, one foot on the bar, waiting for Manning.

Duke stopped midstep as they continued to stare each other down, expressionless. A few men near Fargo noticed the direction of his gaze and looked to see Manning's returned stare. They backed away, and as more and more people noticed, the room cleared with a sudden clatter of overturned chairs. After a long moment, Manning continued down and walked slowly up to Fargo.

"Where's the girl?" Manning asked.

"Upstairs." Fargo's eyes were as cold as steel knives.

Manning was surprised for a moment and then recovered himself. He smiled very slowly.

"Plenty more where she came from." Manning cocked his head to one side as he looked down from his huge height to the Trailsman. "You've been getting in my way, little man," Manning said.

"Guns or bare hands?" Fargo asked.

Manning reached down and slowly unbuckled his belt, and slung it onto the bar. For an instant, Fargo's rage made him consider shooting the unarmed man, and he hesitated just an instant, and then unbuckled his belt as well.

Manning led the way out the batwing doors and onto the street. The sun was just setting, splashing the clouds blood red. The crowd poured out of the bar behind them, and Fargo heard one man taking bets and laying odds. It was two to one. Duke to win.

They stripped off their hats and faced off, knees bent, dancing in the dusty street.

Manning was the size of a grizzly bear, Fargo thought, with arms and legs like the trunks of trees. Fargo kept his eyes on Manning's face. He couldn't win on strength alone. He knew that. He'd have to outsmart him. Find his one weakness and go for it.

They circled each other in icy silence. The crowd around them grew. Fargo's eyes never left Manning's. But he felt a small prick of doubt that Manning had any weakness at all.

Duke stepped forward and threw a punch into the air. Fargo leapt aside and closed in, delivering a hard left to Duke's ribs. He heard a slight crack and knew he'd connected. He danced back and eyed Manning, whose eyes blazed black.

Manning closed in, his right guarding his face, and threw a left, down low, but Fargo dodged it, spinning around and bringing his two elbows hard into Manning's kidneys. Duke roared and staggered away a few steps, bent over. Somebody in the crowd offered to bet even odds. Fargo smiled to himself.

Maybe, just maybe, he had discovered Manning's weakness. He was a huge man. But he didn't move fast. Fargo realized he could spin in, deliver a few hard punches, and get away before Duke could land one on him. So far, so good.

Manning had now straightened up, fury in his eyes. He blindly ran toward Fargo, like a charging bull. Manning struck out, catching Skye's jaw with a painful glancing uppercut that made the sky above explode.

Fargo jumped aside. His jaw wasn't broken, but if Manning had scored a direct hit, it would have been. Hell, Manning packed a lot of weight in his fists.

Fargo wheeled about, as Manning came around again. Just as he neared, Fargo ducked another punch and put out his foot. Manning sprawled onto the ground, and Fargo threw himself on top of the huge man. Fargo used all of his strength to grasp one of Duke's huge arms, pinning it behind his back and slowly forcing it upward. The crowd cheered. Fargo held Manning down for a full minute while he struggled and then finally relaxed. Fargo got up. All around him, men were paying up their bets. The fight was over.

Manning rolled over on his back, and Fargo offered his hand to pull him to his feet, but Manning jerked him downward. Fargo stumbled forward, finding himself suddenly down on the ground. Duke rolled on top of him and began pounding him with heavy fists like steel mallets.

Fargo squirmed to get away as the blows rained down on him, and he felt his nose crunch, and his ears ringing. Summoning all his strength, Fargo suddenly shot his fist upward into Manning's belly. It was an impossible punch, but it caught Manning's lower ribs, which snapped inward, and the breath left him. The blows ceased, and Manning rolled off of him.

Fargo got to his knees, shaking his bloodied head. The blows had done him damage, and it was hard to see straight. Suddenly he heard a roar from the crowd and caught sight of Manning's feet coming for him and his boot being drawn back. Fargo vaulted to one side just in time, and Manning, his foot unexpectedly kicking empty space, lost his balance and went down on his back.

Fargo got to his feet, and the crowd laughed and clapped approvingly. Manning lay still for a long moment, and Fargo thought he might have been knocked unconscious. But then he blinked several times, and shaking his head, he got to his feet.

"Had enough?" Fargo asked.

Manning crouched down in answer. He slid one of his hands into his pants pockets for a moment in an odd gesture. Then removed it. His fists were clenched and his face dark with anger.

He came for Fargo again, running like a huge buffalo, head down. Once again, Fargo waited until the last moment and then stepped aside, but this time Manning was ready. At the last instant, his huge arm shot out and caught Fargo across the neck, pulling Duke around him so that he held Fargo in his iron grip. His right fist was coming in again and again, and Fargo felt sudden pain, not the pain of blows, but a deeper, hot pain. And he realized Duke had a small knife in his fist.

The realization gave Fargo a sudden burst of energy, and in an instant he wrenched himself sideways so that the blows fell along his shoulders, cutting and cutting him. He ducked his head and concentrated on delivering blows to Manning's midsection, which was all he could reach. For a moment, he thought of retrieving the knife from his ankle strap, but there was no way he could reach it. He felt himself weakening as the hot blood bathed his side.

"Knife! Knife!" he heard some of the men call out from the crowd. "Unfair!"

But the voices came from a long distance away. And as his knees gave way, he opened his eyes once more to see Manning's grinning face above him, and then his boot pulled back and Fargo braced himself for the exploding pain and colors. All went black.

"You're damn lucky to be alive," Sylvia said, leaning over the bed and bathing his face with cool water. "Manning thought he'd killed you when he ran. And so did I."

Fargo could only open one eye and that one partway. Sylvia's pretty face above him was slightly out of focus. He moved his hand to his face and felt the bandages, the swollen eye, the lumps on his head. He glanced at the window and saw that it was dark outside.

"Nothing broken," Sylvia said. "And that's a miracle."

Fargo tested his limbs slowly, stretching them despite the pain shooting along every nerve in his body. He felt the hard bandages all along his side where Manning had used his knife.

"That bastard," Sylvia said. "He cut you up pretty bad. Doc said you were leaking bad as a water barrel in a shooting range. Took more thread to sew you up than it takes to make a dress."

Fargo forced the corners of his mouth to go up slightly to show Sylvia that he appreciated her talk. And her care.

Shit, he hurt in places he didn't even know he had, he thought. He closed his eyes again and slept.

A while later, he awakened again. The sun came splashing through the curtains. It felt like morning, he thought. His head felt clearer. The pain was still with him, all over, but he could push it away. He summoned his strength and pushed himself onto his elbows. He glanced down and noticed they had put him in a nightshirt.

"Skye!" Sylvia rose from a rocker where she had been sitting across the room. "You lie back down there on that bed!"

He grinned up at her and shook his head. He gritted his teeth and, ignoring the screaming pain, forced himself to sit up and swing his legs over the edge of the bed. His body obeyed him, but his head roared.

He opened his mouth to say "I'm fine," but the words didn't come. He had to lick his dry lips and swallow a few times before he could make himself heard.

Sylvia had crossed the room and stood beside him, holding a glass of water. He accepted it gratefully and then found it easier to talk.

"How long have I been here?"

"Two days. You were out cold."

Fargo nodded. Two days. Manning could be anywhere by now. And Broken Bow and Black Finger had had their meeting.

"How's Gina?" he asked.

"Fine," Sylvia said. "She cried about Duke for a whole night. Then she cheered up a bit. She asked me a lot of questions about men. And about you in particular." Skye gave Sylvia a wan smile. "Yesterday, she decided she wanted to go back to her father," Sylvia continued. "But then we got word that the Indians are gathering out on the plains. Some of the hunters told us they heard that there had been some meeting between the chiefs and they've declared war. Apparently, Brimwell panicked and sent word to Straver to bring the troops back. But that will take a week. Anyway, it isn't going to be safe out there for a while, so Reggio's coming here to be with his daughter until things calm down."

Fargo nodded. Damn it. So, the tribes would start fighting each other again. It was going to be a bloody mess.

There was a knock at the door, and a pretty redhead in a lavender day dress entered, bringing a bowl of soup. Her eyes widened in surprise to see him sitting up, and she smiled widely.

"That damn Duke Manning," the redhead said. "Why, you had him beat until he started using that knife on you. Once you went down, a few of the men tried to get him, but he got away. Too bad the sheriff wasn't in town. Of course, since he didn't kill you, he'd probably just have gotten a night in jail."

Fargo nodded and took the soup from her hands.

"Thank you, Prissy," Sylvia said. So this was the one Manning had been with, Fargo thought.

"I especially wish you'd gotten that bastard," Prissy said. "He managed to talk me into a double, and then instead of paying like he was supposed to, he left me a smelly old buffalo robe. Now what am I going to do with that? I guess I can sell it."

Fargo started and looked up at her.

"Can I see it?"

Prissy stared disbelievingly.

"The buffalo skin? Sure."

In a moment she had brought it back into the room and Fargo turned it over on his lap. It was well tanned, Indian fashion, and there in the center were the three small holes pierced through the hide.

Fargo stared at the markings and knew that he was holding the proof of what he had always suspected. Manning had probably taken the robe from the Cheyenne Fargo had found freshly killed on the way into town with Gina. He had been right. Manning was responsible for the killings of the Cheyenne. And probably the Kiowa, too. But why?

"Can I buy this from you?" Fargo asked, fingering the skin.

"Oh hell, just keep it," Prissy muttered. "I don't

even want to have it around. It smells like Duke."
She left the room.

Sylvia was watching Fargo's face carefully.

He put a hand out to the bedstead and then slowly rose to his feet.

"I have to go," he said quietly.

"After Manning?" Sylvia said. "In your condition? That would be suicide."

Fargo took a stumbling step forward. He ground his teeth against the pain shooting through every joint. His head swam.

"Oh hell," he muttered. "I have to." He took a faltering step toward the door.

Sylvia planted herself in front of him and put her hands on both hips.

"One more day of recuperation, Skye," she said firmly. "I insist." She reached out and pushed him firmly down on the bed and headed toward the door. "Now, lie down and rest. I'll be back later."

Sylvia swept out of the door. Then Fargo heard the key in the lock. Goddamn her. She had locked him in. For his own good, of course.

But it couldn't wait. If it took every ounce of his strength, he would go after Manning and go after him now. It took a long time for Fargo to struggle out of the nightshirt and into his clothes, which he found hanging on pegs. When he was fully dressed, he bent down and picked up the buffalo robe. Then he slowly limped across the room toward the window.

He looked out. Perfect. His room was in the rear overlooking the stables. And no one was in sight.

He had to summon his strength even to lift the window sash. Then he slowly and painfully crawled out onto the sun-warmed tin roof, which sloped gently down. He threw the robe down to the ground, then slid to the gutter, grasped the edge of it, and let his long lean body down, hanging in space for an instant. As he dropped onto the balls of his feet, crippling red pain shot through his feet and legs. He staggered for an instant, then regained his balance, retrieved the robe, and headed across the yard to the stable.

The Ovaro whinnied when it smelled him approach. He balled up the robe and put it in one saddlebag, finding his Colt inside. He strapped it on.

He mounted the Ovaro quickly, ignoring his body's agony. His head whirled. The pinto walked slowly out of the yard. He turned onto the dusty street and put the pinto into a gentle canter, heading out of town.

During the first few miles, Fargo kept the Ovaro in a smooth, slow gait. Nevertheless, he had to fight back the waves of anguish as his beaten, wounded body jostled up and down with the motion of the horse. He worried that the wounds from Manning's knife might break open and leak. He slipped his fingers beneath the bandages and felt the tight stitches along his side. He'd be all right.

By the time the sun was high, he felt better, enjoying the cool autumn wind at his back and the warmth of the sun. His mind was suddenly at peace and his thoughts distinct.

Manning had almost destroyed Sylvia. And Gina. And Reggio. And the Cheyenne and Kiowa, too. Fargo no longer felt the rage well up inside him. Instead, it was a cold and calculating need to see justice done. He was riding out to find Manning. Fargo kept his mind devoid of thought as he put the pinto into a gallop. He no longer felt the pain, his mind centered entirely on the image of Duke Manning.

It was midafternoon when he came across the Cheyenne scouts. He spotted them several miles to the north of him, and he headed that way. They sat waiting for him as he approached.

The three braves sat tall on their ponies. As Fargo galloped nearer, he saw their muscled bodies gleaming with war paint in yellow, white, and red. A profusion of eagle feathers fell from their headbands, and otter tails dangled from their long lances. Their ponies were bridled with a trailing rawhide thong so that if they fell, they might grab the thong and slow their horse to remount. An unhorsed rider was a dead man in the heat of battle. Their coup sticks were striped like barbers' poles. He recognized Yellow Dog.

"You fight today?" Fargo asked, raising his hand in greeting.

"We will meet the Kiowa here soon," Yellow Dog answered. "It is time for my tribe to fight again under the sky. The Kiowa are now our enemies."

"Then Black Finger and Broken Arrow could find no peace?"

"They are two old men," said Yellow Dog. "While they talked by the creek, another of our braves was killed by Kiowa. The peace is gone. Soon we will call our friends the Arapaho to help us fight. Then the old days of warriors will return!"

Yellow Dog lifted his lance toward the sky and let out a bloodcurdling cry.

The sound was swallowed by the vastness of the plain and then, from far to the south, Fargo heard an answering wail. He turned and saw, along the horizon, a thin, dark line that appeared and then moved across the plain toward them, wavering with the rills but never breaking. A hundred Kiowa braves, he reckoned. He turned to look back at the three Cheyenne and saw that an equal number of their own warriors had appeared in the north, making their way across the prairie.

In a few moments, the ground he stood on would be a killing field, bloody with the fresh dead of both tribes. And all caused by Manning. He felt sure of it. But he still did not understand why Manning would kill for a couple of buffalo robes. He threw the question away and looked again at the oncoming lines of warriors.

He could hear their cries distinctly now, wavering on the afternoon wind. Both lines advanced slowly. They would come nearer and then begin galloping forward in the final charge.

"It is a good day to die," Yellow Dog said, and he turned away toward his own line.

If he had any sense, Fargo thought, he would get the hell out of here, but he felt rooted to the spot, watching the oncoming lines of Indians.

Maybe, he thought, it was his quarter Indian blood that would not let him leave. He heard the song of war rise in him as the tribes approached. But he wanted the killing to stop.

What would halt them? What would make them

listen, at last, to reason? What would make them see that their real enemy was a large white buffalo hunter who lied to them both?

The lines of warriors came on. They had spotted him, on his horse, on the prairie between them, and some of them pointed wonderingly. In center of each of the lines rode the chiefs, their wide and long eagle feather war bonnets marking them even from this distance.

Fargo had the thought that if he could just get them to talk together one more time, with the aid of the buffalo skin Manning had given Prissy, he could avert the bloodshed. He rode forward.

Suddenly, he sighted a small hillock and rode toward it. He dismounted, pulled the buffalo robe from the saddlebag, and slapped the Ovaro's rump so that it cantered some distance away.

Skye Fargo stood on the top of the rise, in the middle of two oncoming lines of warriors. Any moment, the Indians would break into a gallop, racing toward one another. The late-afternoon light slanted across the grass.

Fargo quickly spread the robe on the grass, skin side up so he could see the markings.

And then he did the first thing that came into his mind.

Skye Fargo began to dance.

Standing on the buffalo robe that Duke Manning had killed for, he lowered his head and his feet began to move in the rhythmic toe and heel motions he knew so well. He had danced the buffalo hunt dance many times when visiting camps of various tribes.

It was hard at first. The fresh pain from the bruises and knife cuts constricted his movements, but still he danced. His body gradually lost its stiffness until he did not feel his wounds at all. He ignored the oncoming Indians, concentrating only on the dance. He pawed the ground like the buffalo, then, fingers on his head like horns, moved in a slow circle, up and down. It was the Indian blood in him, he thought, that made it feel so natural. And he danced on, thinking of nothing but the buffalo.

Suddenly, he became aware that time had passed. The sun had lowered, the light had turned soft gold. Fargo knew the dance was over. He slowed and lifted his hands to the sky in what the Indians believed was the final asking for the buffalo to come. When he brought his arms down, he was looking at Black Finger who stood ten feet away watching him.

Fargo glanced around and saw Broken Bow, leaning heavily on his lance, standing on the opposite side of the hillock. The warriors of both tribes sat silently on their ponies in long lines, facing one another across the plains.

"Why do you make the sacred buffalo dance on this place of battle?" Broken Bow asked. "We cannot kill each other now for fear the buffalo god would be angry."

"Because you fight the wrong enemy," Fargo said. He motioned to the chiefs to walk up the rise and join him.

"We fight the Kiowa," Broken Bow said. "They are our enemy now. Yesterday, we found Gray Wing murdered. His buffalo robes were gone. And his weapons. A Kiowa arrow was in him."

"But why would the Kiowa warriors leave a valuable arrow? And why would they take Cheyenne weapons away?" Fargo asked Broken Bow. "Why would Kiowa warriors not take the scalps of their enemies?"

Broken Bow looked at Black Finger for a long time.

"The Kiowa would not do these things," Fargo said.

"But my braves saw these things," Broken Bow said.

The Kiowa chief nodded.

"We have wondered these things, too, about the Cheyenne. But our eyes saw Cheyenne weapons in our braves."

"Then use your eyes to see this," Fargo said. "Yesterday, the white hunter Duke Manning gave this robe to a woman in town." Fargo gestured down at the robe lying skin up on the grass. Broken Bow knelt down and looked closely with his milky eyes. Fargo wondered if he could make out the three small holes piercing the hide.

"That is a Cheyenne robe," said Broken Bow, getting to his feet. "Marked the way you taught us." He was thoughtful. "But why would our friend the white hunter kill us?" he mused. "And the Kiowa?"

"And why would he take our weapons?" Black Finger cut in.

"I don't know yet," Fargo said. "But I intend to find out."

Broken Bow nodded slowly, his clouded eyes never leaving Fargo. He stood in his war paint, leaning on his feathered lance.

"I see the truth now," Broken Bow said, slowly nodding. "I see this skin with Cheyenne marks. And I see we fight the wrong enemy."

Black Finger nodded agreement.

"Today is not the day to die," Broken Bow said.

Black Finger said, "It is a good day to track a big white hunter. All of our warriors are here." He grinned and made a sweeping gesture toward the lines of braves.

"Our warriors will join together," said Broken Bow. "Together we will make war on the big white hunter who has taken our buffalo skins and killed our braves. We will fight together!"

Fargo raised his hand, and they both looked at him.

"Wait a minute," said Fargo. "If you kill white men—Duke Manning and his hunters—the army will come after you. There will be more bloodshed. The army will not understand why you have killed Duke Manning. They will only see the dead bodies of whites killed by Indians."

The Indian chiefs looked at one another and nodded slowly.

"Where is Duke Manning now?" Fargo asked.

"He is heading east," Black Finger said. "One half day away. Many buffalo are there. Tomorrow he is hunting."

Fargo nodded, a plan taking shape in his mind. He smiled very slowly.

"Then tomorrow we'll go buffalo hunting, too," he said.

It was near noon on the following day when Skye Fargo reined in on the top of the rise and gazed across the vast prairie, which dipped down into a gentle bowl. Half of the wide valley was golden grass, the other half a dark mass of grazing buffalo. The huge herd blanketed the opposite hillside. The thousands of bison were nearly motionless, intent on feeding. An occasional movement, caused by a running calf or a complaining cow, rippled across the sea of buffalo backs. It was impossible to judge how large the herd was, since it stretched up the slope and out of sight beyond the crest of the distant hill.

But Fargo knew the Cheyenne and the Kiowa were riding quietly right now around the bison, seeking the opposite side, the upwind side, of the herd.

He patted the bandages on his side again. Not bad. He had spent the evening in the Cheyenne camp. Broken Bow's tribe had welcomed him and the Kiowa warriors. After feasting and discussing their plans, Ten Claws had administered new herbal dressings to his stitched wounds. And had found other ways to make him feel better. He smiled at the memory as his eyes followed the ragged edge of buffalo.

Then he spotted them. Almost two miles distant and downwind from the herd. A small dark smudge on the edge of the huge, dark shifting shape.

Their horses were tethered far up the slope, some distance away from the hunters. Duke Manning and his men were dark dots creeping along the edge of the herd on foot. They were moving slowly and stealthily, plunging a row of forked sticks into the ground and propping the long buffalo guns into them, aimed straight at the bison.

Gunfire alone would usually not start a buffalo stampede. It was the smell of blood that maddened them and started the buffalo running. From the downwind side and using heavy Sharps buffalo rifles and heavy caliber ammunition, a good hunter could shoot seven or eight buffalo by the time the herd began to stampede in the opposite direction, away from the smell of blood. So, with his crew of a dozen men, Manning could down almost a hundred buffalo before they turned tail.

Fargo glanced up at the sun. It was almost midday. The timing was going to be tricky, he thought. The plan just might fail. And if it did, he'd die.

He let the Ovaro move slowly across the hillside toward the spot where Manning's men had left their horses tethered. Just as he reached the horses, he saw that he'd been sighted. One of Manning's crew strode up the hillside toward him.

Fargo dismounted quickly and left the Ovaro untethered. He walked uphill of the horses, so that their bodies hid him from the men below. He quickly loosened their pickets. He patted the Ovaro's muzzle as he came around it to meet the man ascending the hill. It was the bald man who had been rolling the loaded dice in the game at Reggio's.

"How's gambling?" Fargo asked.

The bald man started when he recognized him.

"What the hell are you doing here?" he asked. "Duke said he beat you to death back in McKinney."

"I don't kill easy," Fargo said.

The bald man surveyed the bare hills all around them.

"You come here alone?"

"What does it look like?" Fargo said.

Fargo glanced at the hunters standing down in the valley at the edge of the herd, near their positioned buffalo guns. Duke Manning, looming over the others, was looking up toward them, shading his eyes with one hand. Fargo doubted he'd been recognized. Yet.

"Duke ain't going to be real happy to see you again," the bald man said, shaking his head. "You're real stupid coming here alone."

Fargo shrugged.

"I came to have a talk with Duke. Got some questions I want answered."

Fargo started down the long slope. The sun was high overhead. Almost midday. A few minutes more, he thought. A few minutes to get some answers.

Duke Manning had recognized him now, Fargo thought as he descended. The big hunter began moving toward him. Fargo was close enough to see now that, as he suspected, none of the hunters was wearing a side arm. Even a good .45 was almost useless against a ton of bison. There were only the huge buffalo guns, propped in the forked sticks.

Fargo hastened forward. He didn't want Manning to get too far from the edge of the herd.

When they were within fifteen feet of each other, they both halted. The bald man walked around Fargo to stand behind Manning. The crew of hunters drew up in a line, watching. None wore guns.

Manning's eyes narrowed.

"Hell, I thought I'd kicked you into hell already," Manning snapped. "Come back for more?"

"Not exactly," Fargo said.

"You been getting in my way, little man," Duke said. His hand twitched, then he looked down and remembered he wasn't armed with his pistol. He tensed and glanced up at Fargo, but it was too late. Fargo drew his Colt from his holster in one fast, fluid motion.

"The first one that moves gets a bullet," Fargo said.

"At most, you got six bullets in that pistol," Duke said. "There are a dozen of us."

"Then half of you will die," Fargo said.

Duke growled as he considered this. The men shifted and glanced at one another warily, but nobody moved.

"Whaddya want anyway?" Duke asked. He removed his hat and mopped his brow, but his dark eyes never left Fargo's.

"Some answers," Fargo said. "You've been causing a lot of trouble around here."

"What? That little girl? She wanted to run away from home," Manning said, shrugging. "Not my fault. She's probably gone back to Reggio. Thanks to your meddling." Manning spit on the grass. "But that bastard humpback'll get over it soon enough. You watch. In a week he'll be trading with me again. He can't afford not to."

"Sure," Fargo said. "And the money Reggio owes you? When do you plan to take over the trading post?"

Manning rubbed his chin.

"What's it to you?" he said. "That's a business deal between me and Reggio."

"And the men you sent to ambush his money coming upriver? And the brown-bearded one you sent to shoot me in McKinney?"

"Don't know anything about that," Manning said in a mocking tone. "And you can't prove I do." Several of the men sniggered and elbowed each other.

"How about the extortion you pulled on Sylvia?"

"She gave me part of her business at The Gilded Cage," Manning said, smiling. "Ain't that sweet of her? And it's strictly legal. You can't pin anything on me."

"Not even killing the Indian hunters?" Fargo asked. "How about that? You've been attacking them, stealing their skins, and leaving weapons around so they'll start another tribal war. Now, why would you go to all that trouble I wonder?"

"Who, me?" Manning asked, the mocking tone still in his voice. "I'm a big pal of those redskins.

148

They like me." The hunters chuckled again and exchanged glances.

"Not anymore, Duke," Fargo said, his voice cold. "The Cheyenne have been marking their skins. The one you gave to that dove at The Gilded Cage had Cheyenne markings on it. Broken Bow saw it. And so did the Kiowa. I guess those Indians aren't going to be real friendly to you and your men now."

Duke's eyes narrowed, and he glanced about him. His big hands clenched and unclenched several times, and his face flushed red. But Fargo could see that Duke didn't want to be the first to attack and the first to get shot. Duke's hands twitched again and suddenly he shot out his arm and grabbed the bald man around the neck, pulling him in front as a human shield. Fargo fired, but the bullet caught Manning in the thigh.

"Goddamn you!" Manning yelled. He stumbled with the impact of the bullet, but maintained his grip on the bald man.

Hell, Fargo thought, he hadn't figured on this. Manning would sacrifice one of his own men to save his own life and to get Fargo. He tried to get a clear shot at Manning, but the big hunter held the bald man in front of him while he hunched behind. The bald man was white as death, his face twisted with fear, and his eyes showed white all the way around the pupils. It wouldn't do a damn bit of good to shoot the bald one, Fargo realized. Manning could use a dead body as a shield just as effectively.

Five bullets left, Fargo thought quickly. He couldn't afford to waste one if there wasn't a clear shot. Behind the hunters, Fargo saw the buffalo at the near edge of the herd shifting at the sound of the shot. The hunters were hesitating for a moment, not knowing whether to rush forward or hang back.

"Get the bastard!" Duke shouted. He stumbled toward Fargo.

The line of men started toward him, and Fargo realized he had lost the gamble. Five bullets. Five dead men. No time to reload, and when they got their hands on him, it would be six dead men.

As the men rushed toward him, Fargo took quick aim and hit a heavy-set man dead center. He dropped in his tracks at the same instant Fargo plugged the second in the chest. The hunters hesitated a moment. One of them turned and fled toward the buffalo guns. Fargo shot him in the back.

Two bullets left now. Duke, hunched behind the terrified bald man, was closing in. Still no clear shot.

Fargo swore and pumped a bullet into a tall one coming fast, just a step away. The man screamed in agony and fell. One shot left.

Suddenly the bald man pitched sideways, and Fargo saw Manning's shoulder clear. He squeezed the trigger and the bullet tore past the bald man and into Manning.

Duke roared with pain and dropped the bald man. Too high, Fargo realized. The bullet had only struck Manning in the shoulder.

Duke clutched at his bleeding shoulder and stumbled forward, dragging his wounded leg. His eyes blazed murder. He pitched forward before Fargo could turn.

Fargo went down under Duke, and they rolled

over and over down the slope. All around him, Fargo heard the hunters shouting encouragement to their leader.

Manning was a tornado of fury and blood, pummeling Fargo with his one good arm. Fargo threw an uppercut and caught Manning's jaw. There was a satisfying crunch as Duke's head snapped back. Then Fargo felt Duke's heavy fist descend on the stitched stab wounds. Excruciating pain exploded along his side.

Manning grabbed him around the neck and Fargo grit his teeth. He hit Manning with all his strength in the belly. The big man loosened his hold, and Fargo rolled away. He blinked. His own blood—or Manning's—clouded his vision.

He started to struggle to his feet and then one of the hunters stepped forward and seized his arm. Then there were two of them, holding him tight. Another stepped forward, a swarthy man with a long mustache. He drew back his fist and punched Fargo in the stomach. Fargo heard a rib crack and his insides moved around. The plains spun and the sun did cartwheels.

When his vision cleared again, he was still standing, being held up on either side by two of the hunters. The others were gathered around. Manning stood before him, still clutching his shoulder, his hand covered with blood.

Fargo's eyes focused beyond Manning on the herd of bison. The gunfire and the fighting had disturbed them. They weren't in a stampede, because they couldn't smell blood. But they were moving away from the hunters, loping up the hillside, the near ones pushing and jostling against the others.

"You're real curious, aren't you?" Manning said, thrusting his face into Fargo's. "You got a lot of questions. Well, since you're going to die now, let me just give you some answers. Me and my men want to make some real money, see. And the only way to do that is to control everything around that's making some money."

"Like the other buffalo hunters?" Fargo asked.

"Hell yes. They have to pay us if they want to sleep safe in their bedrolls at night. Pretty soon we're going to own the trading post. And The Gilded Cage. And every goddamn card game in the territory. And if I can trick these stupid redskins into wiping each other out, then we'll have the whole territory and all the buffalo to ourselves."

"So," Fargo said, "you'll control it all—hunting grounds, hunters, trading post, gaming house, and gambling. And you'll take your cut. And a big one."

"This territory is going to make us all very rich men in a year or two," Manning sneered. "And, when Kansas becomes a state, well, they'll be needing a governor. I fancy I'd make a fine first governor."

Manning drew himself up to his full height and raked the fingers of his good hand through his dark hair. It would probably work, Fargo thought as he looked Manning over. That is, if Manning lived.

"But now, you're going to die," Duke said with a smile. "Real slow. This is going to give me great pleasure, Mr. Fargo."

Manning stepped closer to Fargo and drew back his fist. The high noon sun beat down and Fargo felt the blood pound in his temples.

Just then Fargo heard a noise, like rustling leaves. It was starting, he knew. The Indians had started them running. Upwind, on the far side of the herd, they had slaughtered dozens of bulls. And now, maddened by the smell of the fresh kill borne on the wind, the buffalo were beginning to stampede.

Manning heard it too. He paused and looked back toward the buffalo. His nostrils flared. The rustling became a rumble.

Fargo pursed his lips and whistled, a distinct low pitch. A pitch that a horse could hear.

"What the hell . . ." The words were out of Duke's mouth just as the realization hit him.

"Stampede!" Duke yelled. "Run for the horses!"

The two hunters released Fargo's arms and started running straight up the hill. Fargo cut away on a diagonal, heading across the slope and away from the hunters.

Behind them, the whole hillside suddenly became a roiling mass of darkness as the panic spread and the buffalo jostled and turned to run straight for them.

The horses high above them on the hillside caught the panic and reared wildly, pulling at their pickets which Fargo had loosened. One by one, they broke free and turned tail, galloping up the hillside away from the stampede. The men screamed with terror as they struggled up the grassy slope.

Only one horse, the black-and-white pinto, galloped down the hill, straight toward the running men. Fargo whistled again and the pinto veered away from them as they tried to capture it. The Ovaro ran toward Fargo.

The thunder of the hooves behind them grew louder, filling the valley. The buffalo had overrun the buffalo guns and were starting up the slope, pouring across the grass, an oncoming line of horns and dark lowered heads. There were only moments before the herd would overtake them. The hunters were scrambling up the bare hillside with nowhere to hide and no chance of out-running the stampeding herd.

"You bastard!" Fargo heard Duke Manning shout from behind him. The big man had stumbled after Fargo and was only a few paces behind. Duke was cursing with the pain from his shot leg as he ran for his life.

The pinto pulled up alongside Fargo and stopped. Fargo grasped the saddle horn, pulling himself half on the horse as it began to gallop. Manning screamed incoherently and jumped for him, grabbing at Fargo's leg.

The Ovaro's powerful hooves beat the turf as it galloped up the slope. Fargo was half on the saddle, Manning clutching his leg and being dragged along. Fargo felt his grip slipping on the saddle horn and the saddle being pulled sideways with the weight of the dragging man. The sturdy pinto was running hard, but the drag was slowing it down. The thunder of the buffalo filled the air.

Fargo looked down and saw Manning clutching at his ankle with his one good arm. Duke's other arm dangled uselessly, the shoulder soaked with blood. Fargo drew his free leg up and kicked Manning square on the wounded shoulder. Duke screamed in agony, lost his hold, and fell to the ground.

Suddenly free of the weight of Manning, Fargo

pulled himself onto the Ovaro and turned to look back. Duke Manning was rolling over on the ground.

Manning struggled to his feet and took a faltering step in Fargo's direction. He raised his fist in the air, a lone defiant figure in front of a wall of oncoming bison. Fargo watched as Duke Manning was hit by the first charging buffalo, which knocked him to one side. He staggered, regained his footing for a second, and then he fell, arms flailing.

The next instant, Duke Manning was gone, swallowed by the surging wave of buffalo, crushed to death under sharp pounding hooves. Fargo glanced along the line of stampede, but the other hunters had disappeared as well. It was over.

As they galloped over the prairie, Fargo worked the saddle upright and settled into it. He patted the neck of the pinto as it ran just ahead of the thundering herd, the miles flying by beneath them, the grass a yellow blur, and the distant horizon stark and unchanging against the clear blue autumn sky.

Soon the buffalo would tire, slow down, stop. Then he would ride away. Back to Fort McKinney. For a while anyway. And then the trail would call him.

But for the moment, the song of the running buffalo was around him and in him. And all he thought and felt was of this tireless running over the endless grassland, at one with the buffalo.

LOOKING FORWARD!

**The following is the opening
section from the next novel in the exciting
Trailsman series from Signet:**

THE TRAILSMAN #140
THE KILLING CORRIDOR

*1860, the untamed corridor of land
from Kansas to Oklahoma, where death rode
a shadowed trail . . .*

There was only a sliver of a moon and that was good. The fort spread out in a double-L shape with deep shadows along some of the walls, and that was good. But there were six sentries and that was bad, and the stockade posts were ten feet high and that was bad. The big man sat silently atop the magnificent Ovaro as he gazed down at the fort below, his lake blue eyes moving slowly back and forth. The fort was not unfamiliar to him. He had visited it before. All he had to do was figure a way to get inside this time.

No major command post such as Kearny or Laramie, Dodge or Wallace, it had been hastily erected to serve as a base for the field camps sent into the Pawnee and Shoshoni country and sometimes down into the Indian territory of Oklahoma. His eyes narrowed, the big man sent the Ovaro carefully down the slope, keeping inside the cover of black oak and scraggly underbrush. The slope led down close to the right side of the fort and they knew how unwise that was when they built it, but it was the most direct path to bring down water from the spring in the hills. Skye Fargo moved the pinto down to the base of the slope and halted where the oak began to thin and the land leveled off.

The right L-shaped side of the fort lay directly in front of him, some six yards of cleared land between him and the stockade posts, and he swung from the saddle, dropped to one knee, and watched the sentry atop the inside walkway pass on his rounds. He waited, counted off seconds as the sentry passed again, counted off another set of seconds on the soldier's second pass. Forty-five seconds on each pass, give or take a half-dozen seconds. The night was still relatively early. If he waited another two hours, the sentry's rounds would be slower. But Fargo didn't want to wait another two hours. He rested as he watched the sentry patrol. Six sentries for the double-L shape of the fort was too few. But General Eakins had always been an overconfident man. Overconfident and devoted too much to army spit-and-polish than the cruel rudiments of warfare in Indian country.

Fargo's lips pursed as he thought back. He'd had two assignments that involved General Eakins, and he'd come to know the measure of the man. The general was not a bad officer, and he didn't just talk about bravery. He was simply stiff-backed and unimaginative, and those were failings that could lead to disaster in a land where there were no rules except kill or be killed. Fargo cut off his thoughts and returned his attention to the nearest sentry. If he were a Pawnee brave, with perhaps two more near-naked braves beside him, he could easily penetrate the fort. A hunting knife or an arrow could silently take care of the nearest sentry and the other one as well.

But he was no Pawnee brave, and he wasn't about to slay a good United States soldier boy serving sentry duty. That meant he'd have a harder time getting into the compound. He rose and took his lariat from the lariat strap on the saddle. He crouched, muscles tensed, watched the sentry turn to begin his patrol, and counting seconds as he did, Fargo raced across the ground and flattened himself against the stockade wall just as the sentry returned. He heard the sentry turn and begin to walk back the other way, and as he rose, Fargo unraveled a length of the lariat, waited again for the sentry to return and start back. He tossed the lariat then, a quick, almost vertical toss, and felt the rope close around the pointed top of one of the stockade poles. Instantly, he was pulling himself up the side of the stockade, using his feet and arms, monkeylike, and he slid one long leg over the top of the stockade, followed with the other, and dropped on his belly in the deep shadows against the posts.

The sentry came toward him, closer, then turned and began his patrol back in the other direction along the walkway. Fargo flipped the end of the lariat from the stockade post and ran on silent, tiptoe steps to the end of the walkway where the wood steps led down into the compound. He reached the last step and crouched on one knee again in the deepest of the shadows, his eyes fastened on the sentry above. He rose when the sentry began to move away again, stayed against the edge of the stockade as he hurried deeper into the compound. There were still lights on in the barracks though one flickered out as he watched, and he saw a light on in the general's quarters.

He walked silent as a cougar on the prowl, past the light, crouched low as he went by the window, and made his way to the second wooden cabin before the officer's quarters began. He stepped to the door, closed one large hand around the knob, and slowly turned and the door opened. He stepped into the cabin where an almost burned-out candle sat atop the stone border of the wood floor afforded a flickering night light. He took three long, silent steps across the room to the open doorway of the adjoining room, stepped inside, and moved silently to where a double bed took up most of the west wall. He halted at the side of the bed and took a silent moment to gaze down at the young woman lying without a sheet or cover over her, a long, slim body stretched out, encased in a blue nightgown that clung to her as a wet leaf clings to a rock.

Fargo put one hand gently over her mouth and

her eyes snapped open, fright in them first, then a slow awareness pushing away the fright as she stared up at him. He drew his hand away. "Surprise," he murmured.

"I'll say," she breathed and sat up, and her arms were encircling his neck, her lips pressed hard against his. She drew back finally, and he lowered himself to the edge of the bed, his eyes taking in her slender face, the perpetually arched eyebrows he always remembered, the straight nose, and sharply etched lips that gave her a slightly arrogant beauty, her dark brown hair falling shoulder length. She leaned back on the palms of both hands, her arms straight, and a tiny smile lighted her dark blue eyes. "I knew you were coming, of course. Father told me. I just didn't expect you to arrive this way," she said.

"Disappointed?" Fargo asked blandly.

"You know better than that," Annabel Eakins said. "Truth is, when Father told me he'd sent for you, I began wondering how we'd manage any time together. From Father's words it seemed this would be a short visit."

"Probably," Fargo said. "That's why I decided to arrive early."

"A wonderful idea," Annabel said, her eyes flicking across him. "You going to stay all dressed like that in a lady's bedroom?"

"Wouldn't think of it," Fargo said and rose and quickly pulled off his gunbelt, then clothes, and saw the young woman's lips parting and her breath growing shallower as she watched the beauty and power of his muscled body take naked shape in front of her. "Everything you remembered?" he asked as he was down to his last piece of clothing.

"Yes, oh God, yes," Annabel Eakins breathed and leaned forward and whisked the blue nightgown off, and Fargo paused to enjoy her slim loveliness. She was as he remembered, also, all slimness with very modest but high breasts with surprisingly large, deep red nipples and large matching areolas. Her rib cage showed and her slenderness allowed for an almost convex little belly and beneath it, a small but dense black nap. Below it, slim legs were not without shapeliness, hips narrow yet completely in keeping with the rest of her. Annabel always had a steel-wire body, and he could feel the vibrations from it as she rose to both knees, her mouth parted, her breath a small, hissing sound.

Fargo shed the last of his clothes and knew he was already erect and throbbing for her. "Oh Jesus," Annabel muttered as her eyes fastened on him, then her hands reaching out, pressing, touching, stroking, clasping as she made tiny little sounds of delight. Her lips came forward, closed against him, around him, kissing, licking, drawing him in. Her high, firm breasts were quivering as she fell back onto the bed, drawing him with her, and then suddenly her arms were around him and her lips seeking his, imploring soundlessly, the words of the flesh. It had always been that way with Annabel, and he still remembered his surprise at her steel-wire tensions that first time. Now she thrust one modest, high, firm little mound into his mouth, moving it there, pushing, half turning, and he took the large, deep red nipple gently between his teeth, and Annabel half-screamed in delight.

He caressed the nipple with his tongue, circled its soft firmness, and felt Annabel's slender legs falling open, closing and opening again, thighs slapping against each other. "Jeez. Jeez," she breathed as her hips rose, held, quivered, waited, and he ran his lips down her slim body, pushed his face into the dense little nap, and her hands closed around the back of his neck to hold him there. "Yes, oh yes . . . oh God, yes," Annabel gasped, and he moved lower as her thighs fell open. He touched the warm, moist portal for a fleeting instant and Annabel screamed, and her hands were clutching at him, pulling at him as her torso leaped upward in spasms. It had always been that way with Annabel, her tightly wound self refusing all slowness, demanding gratification at once.

Her hands dug into his buttocks, pulling at him, her slim legs rising up to clasp themselves around him, the senses making their demands, the entreaties of the flesh, and he moved to her, sinking smoothly into the warm moistness of her. Annabel's scream was a sigh of ecstasy. "Oh yes, oh yes . . . ah . . . aaaah," she gasped out as she lifted her slender form with a newfound strength, carrying him with her, falling back, and thrusting forward again, meeting his own throbbing lunges. He let himself go, the body remembering its own meetings, and she began to scream as her climax came with its usual speed, her legs stiffening, tightening around him, and her hands pulling him down to the small, high breasts. She was rocketing with him, the sensory burstings that were forever the same yet forever different, and she screamed into his chest, her teeth biting his flesh until suddenly her quivering, shaking spasms ceased and she was still with a sudden stillness.

He stayed with her until with a burst of breath she fell back onto the bed and her legs unclasped from around him. "Oh God, oh my God," Annabel Eakins breathed. He slid from her and lay down beside her, and she turned at once, the high, firm breasts rubbing into his chest. "You know what that was," she murmured.

"An undress rehearsal," he said, and she laughed, a low, husky sound.

"Yes. You know I can't help it the first time," she said. She put her torso half over him, lay with her face against his chest for a few silent minutes, and then lifted her head to meet his gaze. He felt her hand creep down to his crotch, take hold of him, and begin to stroke, caress, slow, tender sensuousness, and he felt himself respond. "Oh yes, oh yes," Annabel murmured in delight as he grew in her hand, and he felt her body shiver in pleasure. She began to make love to him again, but this time the wild, headlong, and heedless passion was replaced by a slower one, no less urgent, no less demanding, but with a new pacing that brought its own excitement.

Only when she neared that moment of ecstasy did the other Annabel assert itself, and her slim body shook and quivered, and her hands dug into him as she pulled his face down to her breasts. Once again, she exploded, and he was ready once again. Her scream was a cry of pure pleasure, all the senses let loose, the flesh triumphing over all else. When she fell back this time, her slim legs stayed clasped around him, holding him to her, the senses unwilling to accept desinence. But finally she let her legs fall away, and he came to lie half over her, his lips brushing one deep red nipple for a fleeting moment, and Annabel's arms circled his neck.

"God, why can't you stop by more often? Why do you wait for Father to call you in?" she asked with an edge of reproach.

"I keep busy. I don't get this way that often," he told her.

"Father thinks highly of you, you know," Annabel said. "He mentioned it again when he told me he'd sent for you."

Fargo's smile was wry. "He might not think so much of me if he knew I was . . . well, here," he said.

"Go on, say it. Screwing his daughter," Annabel finished. "His engaged daughter."

"That still on?" Fargo asked with some surprise. "You and Lieutenant what's-his-name?"

"Whitmore, Lieutenant Whitmore," Annabel said. "You needn't be so surprised. You've never liked Charles." Fargo shrugged his admission. "Charles has many good qualities. He's earnest, sincere, well mannered, dedicated, and a gentleman."

"Go on, finish," Fargo said. "Add dull and a little stupid."

"That's not nice," Annabel half pouted.

"No, it's not, but it's true," Fargo said. "Besides, he's not man enough for you."

She fastened him with a cool stare. "Are you going to take me away?" she asked tartly. "I think we've been through that." He said nothing and there was nothing to say. "I don't have a lot of choice, do I, following Father from one command post to another. Been doing it ever since Mother died."

"I just think you can do better," Fargo said.

"Maybe I will. I'm engaged, not married," she said.

"You're not engaged, not the part of you that counts," he laughed.

"I am when you're not around," Annabel said accusingly. "At least I try harder."

"Want me to go?"

She punched his chest with one small fist as her lips found him again. "The word is come," she murmured and proceeded to make her answer real, and when finally he again lay beside her and watched her slim body cease its quivering, he took her in his arms.

"I've got to leave. It'll be dawn in an hour," he said. "When we meet tomorrow it'll be formal time."

"We've handled that before," she said. "It's kind of fun, knowing we know something nobody else does."

"You've too much of the hoyden in you, Annabel Eakins," Fargo said as he pushed from her and began to pull on his clothes. She walked to the door with him, her slim nakedness a tease, he knew. "Jezebel," he muttered.

"To inspire you to find another time for us before you go," she said.

"That might not be in the cards this time," he said. "But I might get back again."

"I'll settle for that only if I have to," Annabel said as he slipped from the room and paused outside, flattened against the wall of the cabin. The fort was silent save for an occasional whinny from the stables. Silent and dark, with the lariat in his hand, he moved quickly in the deepest shadows, back to the steps that led up to the walkway. He halted at the top step to watch the sentry. The soldier was still making his rounds, but he was moving considerably slower now, taking a full minute to complete his circuit.

Once again, Fargo waited, counted off seconds, and this time dropped the end of the lariat over the pointed top of a stockade post and quickly swung himself over the side. He slid quickly down the rope, touched the ground on the balls of his feet, and jiggled the rope until it came off the top of the stockade post. He let the rope fall to the ground as he pressed himself against the bottom of the stockade, the sentry's footsteps directly above him. He'd taken too long to free the rope. Another second and the soldier would have spotted the lariat around the post top.

Fargo waited and listened to the soldier retracing his steps on the walkway before he darted across the cleared land and into the line of oaks. He retrieved the Ovaro, led the horse slowly up the hillside, and when he reached the top, the first pink-gray light of dawn touched the distant horizon. He found a deep cluster of black oak, took off his shirt and lay down where the new sun would only filter through. He let himself sleep a few hours, found a small stream, and washed and let the Ovaro drink. It was a little past the midday hour when he rode through the open gates of the fort. He paused as a platoon of troopers rode past him on their way out of the fort. He saw the smooth, earnest face of Lieutenant Whitmore in the lead. Whitmore saw him, nodded to him, and led his squad on, his sandy hair protruding from the rear of his cap.

The fort was a busy place now, horses being groomed, foot soldiers taking drill, visitors from wagon trains that halted outside the compound moving through the area. He dismounted in front of the general's quarters, the command flag on a short flagpole, marking the place. Not that he needed that to know. General Edmund Eakins came from his office to meet him, his tall, gray-haired form as trim as always, his long face breaking into a welcoming smile, blue eyes with a tiny twinkle in them. The general might not be terribly imaginative, but there was an old-fox quality about him that was very much there and he ran a tight command.

"Glad you're here, Fargo. It's been a while," the general said as he led the way into his office, a modest room with a steel desk that doubled as a living room, a sofa and chairs taking up the other end. A slim figure stepped from an adjoining room looking bandbox fresh in a yellow shirt and a dark blue skirt. "You know Annabel, of course," the general said, and Annabel flashed a charming smile.

"Of course," Fargo said.

"I've some ice coffee made. Can I get you a glass, Fargo?" Annabel asked.

"Yes, I'd like that," Fargo said. "How've you been, Annabel?" he asked.

"Doing my best," Annabel smiled cheerfully, and he wondered if the general caught the added amusement in her eyes.

"Sit down, Fargo. I'll spell it out as best I can, which isn't very much," General Eakins said. "I got orders to contact you for a special assignment."

"For the army?"

"Not exactly. Yes and no," Eakins said, and Fargo frowned. "There's a man who needs a trailsman, someone with your talents. The army has orders to help him in any way it can. His name is Arthur Brenner, and he's a Pinkerton agent."

"A Pinkerton man?" Fargo echoed in surprise.

"That's right. The government has used Pinkerton men on a number of cases. This appears to be one more of them."

"But they didn't tell you what it's all about?"

"No, except that it might have some bearing on the increased Indian activity we've had. The Pawnee, in particular, have been raiding wagon trains with increasing regularity. In fact, we escort some trains as far as we can and advise others not to go out without extra outriders."

"They been raiding your patrols?" Fargo queried.

"Skirmishes mostly, but they're getting bolder. And there seem to be more of them. I don't like it and I've added patrols as a show of strength."

"They hit any settlements?" Fargo asked.

"Yes, a few, north toward the Nebraska Territory," the general said as Annabel appeared with the ice coffee. She sat down to listen after Fargo took his glass, and Eakins went on with his briefing. "This Pinkerton man knows all of it, and of course he'll fill you in. Leastwise I'd think so, though they can be very close-mouthed."

"Where do I find him?" Fargo asked.

"Northeast, not far from the Missouri border. There's a town called Creeksville."

"I know the place," Fargo said.

"He has a cottage a mile or so west of the town, up in a low hill of hackberry. I understand it's the only place on that hill," the general said.

"You know what he looks like? You ever meet him?" Fargo questioned.

"No, but I was furnished a description. Five ten, middle-aged, balding, stocky build. Large nose and a high voice," Eakins answered.

"That'll do," Fargo said, downed his ice coffee, and rose to face Annabel. "Good to see you again," he said, and she returned a wide smile.

"I'll walk out with you, Fargo," the general said, and he went all the way to the stockade gate, where Fargo swung onto the Ovaro. "Good luck. The army wouldn't have had me track you down if this wasn't something special. You're a man of special talents, Fargo," the general said, and he smiled up at him reflectively. "It takes a man of special talents to sneak into my fort and sneak out again without ever touching one of my sentries or being seen by them. Good luck again."

The general spun on his heel and strode away, and Fargo realized his jaw was hanging open. He swallowed hard as he pulled it shut and stared after the tall, trim, receding figure. The thoughts flew through his mind. Should he follow after the man and ask questions? Should he make his way back and tell Annabel what had been said? But the questions flew away at once. He'd do nothing, he knew, as he watched the general's back disappear into his quarters.

Fargo spurred the Ovaro forward at a walk. "I'll be goddammed," he muttered as he rode from the fort and realized he was in something close to a state of shock.

There's an epidemic with 27 million victims. And no visible symptoms.

It's an epidemic of people who can't read.

Believe it or not, 27 million Americans are functionally illiterate, about one adult in five.

The solution to this problem is you... when you join the fight against illiteracy. So call the Coalition for Literacy at toll-free **1-800-228-8813** and volunteer.

Volunteer Against Illiteracy. The only degree you need is a degree of caring.